STORIES FROM GLIMMER VALE

Volume One

MICHAEL KINGSWOOD

CONTENTS

ABOUT THIS BOOK

This is a collection of five short stories that are set in the world of the Glimmer Vale Chronicles.

Legacy and Hidden Magic explore the back stories of Selam, who plays an important role in Glimmer Vale, and Melanie, who is prominent throughout the series.

Wedding Gifts and Lost Credit feature Julian and Raedrick, the series' central characters, on adventures in and around Glimmer Vale's primary town of Lydelton.

Captive Hearts explores events outside of, but related to and impacting on the people living in, Glimmer Vale.

Enjoy the book! After you're done, please come to Michael's website and sign up for his mailing list at michaelkingswood.-com/newsletter-signup/. Guaranteed to be spam free, he uses it to announce new releases and special promotions for his fans.

MAP OF GLIMMER VALE

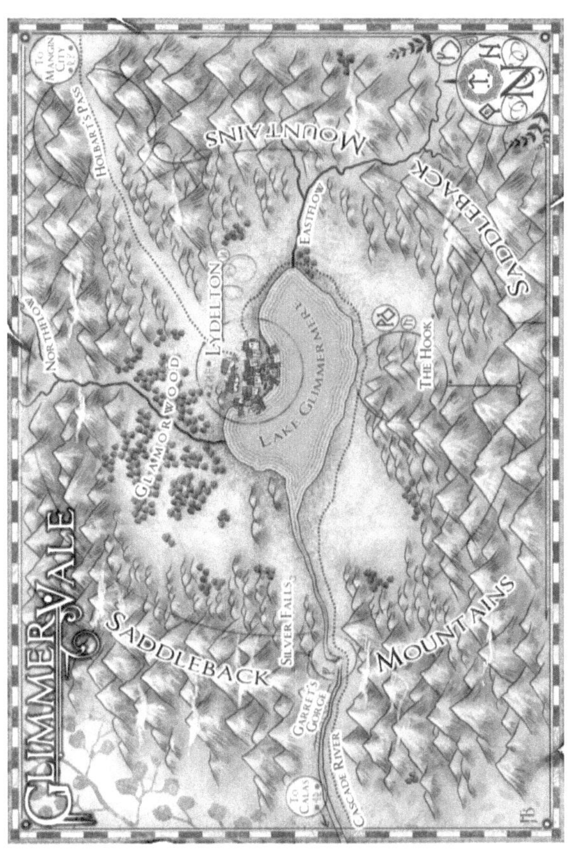

LEGACY
A Glimmer Vale Chronicles story

MICHAEL KINGSWOOD

AUTHOR OF *THE PERICLES CONSPIRACY*

LEGACY

Selam's most prized possession, a master-crafted sword passed down from father to son for generations, represents the totality of his family's history and greatness.

But Selam's brother has a different view. And with the family business teetering on the edge of ruin, they must decide where their family's true legacy lies.

Legacy takes place before Glimmer Vale (Glimmer Vale Chronicles #1).

The sky was burning crimson on the eastern horizon. The sun's disk was a third of the way gone, down into her nighttime abode, and rays of red-orange streamed down through gaps in the partial cloud cover like spotlights, illuminating here and there bits of the rolling grassland before the ridge where Selam stood just a little bit brighter than the others. Some last remnants of light against the encroaching blackness, hanging or just a little bit longer than their fellows, despite the fell cast to that illumination.

He shuddered, drawing his fine blue silk-cotton cloak tighter around his body despite a lack of physical chill. He watched the orb lower further past the hill lands east of his home, and couldn't help but consider that he could relate to those little swaths of land, seemingly desperately clinging to whatever light they could.

The swish of grass behind him brought Selam out of his reverie, and his hand went to the well-worn leather that wrapped the grip of his sword, master crafted by Farelio himself and handed down to him from his father as had been done for generations in his family.

Without thinking about it, he bent his legs slightly, his muscles bundling as they tensed, ready to spring into action.

But then the smell of horse and pipe tobacco reached his nose, along with a sweet-sour that he would recognize anywhere.

"Good evening, brother," Selam said, as he relaxed in his stance.

The movement from behind him stopped, and Selam could imagine the look on Hafi's face. He was Selam's senior, but not as skilled in the martial ways. He always was surprised when Selam saw the obvious traces and signs that he himself missed.

A rueful chuckle, and then Hafi stepped up beside Selam on his left. Hafi shook his head, his long, black hair swaying in time with his movement and his lips drawing upward into a wry grin, white teeth flashing stark contrast with the blackness of his beard.

He was of a height with Selam, but plump about the middle. He wore his robes loosely, white and brown cotton that hung down to his ankles and would restrict his movement if it came down to a fight.

But Hafi had never been one for the great contest. That's why he had inherited their father's business, and Selam the sword.

"How do you always know it is me?" Hafi asked.

Selam sniffed. "The cologne you wear. Its southern spices are… unique, here." And more than a little excessive, he didn't say.

Hafi half-chuckled again, and raised a meaningful eyebrow Selam's way. "The ladies of Tyrash certainly appreciate it."

"One wife is not sufficient for you? Would you seek two more? Three?" Selam had lost track of how many mistresses Hafi had these days. And really didn't want to know.

The humor went out of Hafi's eyes, and his lips compressed into a scowl for a moment. But instead of replying, he looked away from Selam toward the setting sun, now barely visible as the last rim of glow against the increasing darkness of the night all around.

Hafi drew a breath. "I met with Farooq today."

The name sent a little tremor down Selam's spine. As the man holding the lion's share of the debt the family business owed, he would have more than a slight influence on their future.

If there was to be any future.

"Not good news, I'm afraid." Hafi rolled his shoulders slightly, then crossed his arms over his chest. "He wants twenty thousand, by next month."

"Twenty thousand? But we only owe fifteen."

Hafi shrugged. "Late fees, and unpaid interest. And…other matters."

Selam looked sidelong at his brother, and Hafi did not meet his gaze. Had Hafi taken to the gambling dens again? Not that it mattered. They couldn't have paid the sum if it had been five thousand.

They were ruined.

Selam looked down, toward the hilt of his father's sword. Still bright, despite the swiftly departing daylight, the pommel seemed to almost glow of its own accord.

More than a dozen generations had born this sword, in wartime and in peace. In wealth and in poverty, but always with honor. Their father had said that as long as it remained in their family, they had a future to be envied, no matter how dark the days might look at the time.

But now, as the first of the stars became clearly visible overhead and the breeze seemed to already have become more cool as night crept over the land, Selam wasn't sure he could believe that.

They were going to lose father's business. Because Hafi was too -

No. He would not pass judgment on his elder brother. Hafi had inherited the business, and the right to direct it as he chose. And in truth he had often asked Selam's input, and he had not objected to Hafi's decisions. For the most part.

But somehow, still here they were. About to lose it all.

He ran the fingers of his left hand over the sword's pommel, and felt a bit of comfort.

Not all.

Selam felt Hafi's gaze on him, and he looked fully at his brother. Hafi's eyes flicked downward quickly, as though he were ashamed to meet his younger brother eye to eye. Then he visibly steeled himself and looked up.

There was no defeat in Hafi's gaze. Unexpected, and when Selam saw that, his heart leapt.

He reached out and clapped Hafi on the shoulder. "We shall overcome this, my brother," he said. "Our family will emerge stronger than ever."

Hafi placed his hand overtop Selam's, where it still rested on the meat of his shoulder, and nodded. "Yes, we will. I have a plan."

Selam raised a questioning eyebrow.

"Meet me at The Red Phoenix at midnight." His lips turned

upward again, into an eager grin. "Tonight, we shall save our family."

<hr>

Selam knew of The Red Phoenix, and had been inside a handful of times. But never for long, and never so late as this.

He had long ago forsook the call of late night debauchery; a true acolyte of the way of the sword did not go down that path. It was destructive to body and spirit, ruining discipline and eating far too much into the day's work.

He was not surprised Hafi frequented the place, and at late hours, however.

Again, the reason Selam had inherited the sword.

The blocky stone of the tavern's building was unadorned. Just a small sign posted above the dark wood of the double doors allowing entrance. In the daylight, it would show a broad-winged bird, wreathed in red flames, rising from a pile of ash, with the tavern's name written in script above the bird's beak.

Now, a few minutes before midnight, the sign was barely visible in the flickering light of the twin burning torches that rested in sconces on either side of the doors. But the sign was unnecessary, to those who knew Tyrash well.

Having grown up here, that included Selam.

Two thick-armed men in plain tunics stood on either side of the entrance doors. The one on the right looked Selam up and down appraisingly, and for a moment he thought the bouncer would try to make trouble. But then he just grunted and jerked his head toward the interior.

It was more well-lit inside by oil lamps hanging from the bare wooden rafters and mounted in holders along the walls. Tobacco smoke wafted over the long, broad common room that made up most of the tavern's first floor, and there was seating for easily a hundred patrons. Ranging from bare-wood benches alongside equally unadorned tables at the front to satin-cushioned divans at the rear, the tavern was equipped to cater to clientele of all levels of wealth.

The central bar was circular, with stations at three positions where serving wenches could sidle up to fill orders, and casks and more delicate flasks containing everything from the most rude ale from the savage wastes to the northeast to the finest wines from the western kingdoms were tended by a trio of bartenders in grey tunics who wore seemingly eternal smiles on their faces.

A trio of dark-haired dancing wenches in sheer silks that barely concealed their charms swayed on a stage off to the left, moving to the beat of a of drummer, a flutist, and a pair of men playing stringed instruments Selam had seen before but didn't know the name of. They produced a fine melody was all he knew; all he cared to know.

A stairway to the upper level was off to the right, and at a round table not far from the base of the stairs Selam spied Hafi.

His brother was standing there, in the same robes he had worn earlier in the night, with a tall, dark-haired youth. He was lean and muscled, and wore more tightly-fitting clothing than his father; the better to move efficiently in.

Selam found his lips turning downward into a scowl as he saw his nephew, lifting a goblet of what could only be wine to his lips. He had been training the lad—barely thirteen now—in the ways of the sword, as was fitting the men of their family.

This was not part of the way.

"Ah, brother," Hafi said as Selam approached, and reached out to grasp him on the shoulder in greeting. "Will you take wine? This is will be a great night."

Selam kept his eyes on his nephew, who swallowed and slowly lowered his cup to the table. He met Selam's eyes for a moment, but only a moment, instead looking down at the table-top, abashed.

"No," Selam said, finally looking at Hafi, who had noted his son's embarrassment and lost some of his enthusiastic expression. "We have business, you said?"

Hafi let go of Selam's shoulder and nodded. Gesturing toward the stairs, he said, "They are waiting for us."

"Who?"

Instead of answering, Hafi turned toward his son. "Misra, your uncle and I have business to attend to. Wait for us here."

Misra nodded, still not meeting Selam's eyes.

Then Hafi turned and ascended the stairs. Selam didn't follow for a moment, just looking at his pupil and unsure what, if anything, to say. Instead, he turned and followed his brother upstairs.

It was more quiet, and less smokey, in the upper level. The stairs emerged into a broad hallway, walled in stone like the rest of the building and floored in the same unpolished material, though covered in red rugs with golden fringes that looked like they were worth a small fortune each.

The hallway took them past a pair of doors stained the same shade as the double doors leading into the tavern proper, then stopped at a third door that looked somehow more ornate than the other two, though Selam could not have said what exactly it was that gave that impression.

Hafi knocked twice, and a moment later the door opened, and Selam followed him inside.

The man sitting on the divan in the center of the room beyond was the largest Selam had ever seen; but not in a righteous way. His fat rolled lasciviously beneath the loose silk of his silver-blue robes, and his jowls swayed grotesquely with every movement of his head. He was bald, his cheeks rouged to make his pale skin seem more pink, and he had small, pig-like eyes that flashed blue in the lamplight.

But despite his slothful, indolent appearance, there was a sharpness in his gaze and an aura of danger about him.

Selam knew him by description, though he had never met the man before, and immediately he felt the hair on the back of his neck stand up.

What sort of deal was Hafi getting them into here?

"Hafi," the man on the divan said. "Good of you to come." He made a vague sort of waving gesture that almost seemed too lazy to be a dismissal.

But the two girls who were lounging on the divan next to him in silks that were even more sheer than the dancers' below, leaning their lithe, young bodies up against his bulk on either side of his frame, immediately sprang to their feet and scampered off through a small doorway off to the left.

The door they exited through was pulled closed by a muscular man in a fighter's tunic, who wore a broad, curved blade on his right hip and who looked at Selam with a frankly assessing gaze.

This was not the only fighting man in the room. Now that he was over his initial surprise at seeing the fat man they were dealing with, Selam noted no less than half a dozen guards standing unobtrusively but alertly in all corners of the square, tapestry-bedecked room.

He was liking this situation less and less, and was just about to pull Hafi by the shoulder to make him leave when Hafi instead stepped directly in front of the fat man and made a half-bow to him.

"Acharo," he said, "thank you for seeing us at this late hour."

The name confirmed Selam's suspicions, and he wanted to leave even more strongly. Acharo had a reputation in Tyrash. Seemly men did not do business with him.

Whatever this was, Selam was certain he wanted no part of it.

"I was about to ask whether you brought it, but I see you have," Acharo said, his gaze leaving Hafi to rest fully upon Selam. And in particular on his left hip. "Farelio's work, you say? If that holds up, you'll get every penny."

Selam froze, and his left hand went to his sword, his thumb wrapping around the metal of the crosspiece to keep it firmly in place within its scabbard.

"Hafi, what is this?" he said, but he already knew, and he turned accusing eyes on his brother.

He didn't even have the grace to look embarrassed. He met Selam's gaze, and said nothing.

"You would sell our father's sword, our family legacy, to this… this - ?" Selam gestured with his right hand toward the grotesque creature lounging before them, unable to give words to his thoughts about the man.

"I would *save* our family legacy," Hafi said, moving a step closer to Selam. "There are less than twenty weapons from Farelio's forge left in the world. That sword is worth ten times what we owe to Farooq, and Acharo will pay it. With that much, we can secure our family's future forever!"

"*This sword* is our family's future," Selam spat back. "Father said - "

"I know what father said," Hafi said with a heat and a spitefulness that Selam had never heard from him before. Then he snorted. "Meaningless words. I'm talking about gold, in our hands. We can buy another sword."

Selam shook his head, and stepped back from his brother. He lowered into a crouch and his right hand found the grip of his sword, baring the first two inches as he twisted his torso slightly.

Acharo sighed, rolling his little eyes toward the ceiling. "Hafi said you might object," he said, "but it hardly matters. The arrangements are already made." He raised his left hand and made a swirling little gesture with it.

The subtlest of sounds from behind announced the movement of a guard that Selam hadn't seen yet.

Moving from instinct, he twisted to his right, drawing and cutting downward even as he got out of reach of the grasping hand that had been reaching for him.

Selam's sword met the guard's arm at the elbow. Blood and forearm both went flying, and the guard stumbled backward against the wall, screaming in sudden anguish as his one remaining hand clamped against the suddenly gushing wound.

Movement erupted all around him.

Guards moved toward him from both sides, drawing steel as they advanced.

Acharo bounded up from his divan with surprising speed and grace for one of his bulk, and headed toward the same door the two girls had vanished through.

And then Selam could spare attention to nothing but the approaching guards.

These first two were clumsy, half trained, and unused to coordinating with each other. Selam easily sidestepped a thrust from the one, and watched as the miss sent the guard stumbling forward into the path of his comrade's cut.

A chagrined shout from the second guardsman mirrored the first's cry of anguish as the blow struck him where the neck meets the shoulder.

Then Selam was dancing around the still-falling man and slipping the tip of his blade into the other's armpit, puncturing lung and heart before moving past him.

Both guardsmen fell behind Selam, and he saw there were only two remaining.

The muscular man who had been eyeing him before was closing the door off to the side, where Acharo had fled, and there were just this pair to face him.

From the looks on their faces, they wished to be just about anywhere else but right there.

Five seconds later, they were off to the next world, and whatever lay in store for them. Hopefully a good reward; despite their fear they were brave men and had met their fate standing up, with all the skill they had.

The fact that their skill was insufficient was not a blemish on their souls; there was always someone better out there.

Breathing deeply but with controlled, steady breaths, Selam turned back around to see Hafi standing where he had been when the confrontation first began.

His eyes were wide, but not from fright or surprise. He had

sparred with Selam many times when they were growing up, seen him fight in actual battle before.

Hafi knew Selam's skill.

No, they were wide with chagrin, anger even.

"You fool!" Hafi spat. "You have ruined us!"

"I? It was not eye who buried himself in debt."

Hafi shook his head. "No, that was father. I tried to tell you, but you wouldn't hear it. He could do no wrong, in your eyes. The gallant swordsman, the noble warrior." Hafi's mouth twisted in disgust. "The spendthrift and the gambler, the whoremonger!"

"The devil you say." Selam found himself advancing on his brother, fiery anger flaring within his soul.

"It's true, brother." Hafi moved to his left, keeping the distance between himself and Selam constant. "He left the business in debt, and it's been all I can do to stop it from going under, for years. Well I can't stop it anymore." His eyes flickered from Selam's face to the sword, then back. "I could have, though. I am the firstborn. The sword should have been mine by right."

"You chose a different path. The sword is -"

"I know what the sword is!" Hafi's shout practically shook the walls. "That's all I ever heard of growing up, all father ever focused on. And what good did it do?" He shook his head, stopping beside one of the fallen guards. "He focused on it so much, he's destined us, destined his grandson, to be paupers."

"Our family has been poor before. We - "

"No," Hafi said. In one quick, smooth motion he crouched down and grasped the fallen guard's sword. "You can delude yourself If you like, but I will not live as a pauper. And neither will Misra."

Then he launched himself at Selam.

Selam was taken aback, both at the ferocity of his brother's attack and by the fact that he was making the attack at all. For a heartbeat, Selam stood still in stunned disbelief.

Then he spun to the side, leaving Hafi's blade to sing through the air where had been moments before.

Selam backpedalled, keeping his sword up at a guard but no more. "Brother, stop," he said. "We can - "

Hafi's feral growl overwhelmed his words, and again Selam had to dodge aside to avoid being skewered.

But Hafi kept on coming, and Selam kept falling back. From somewhere beneath the sounds of their fight, below the moans of the loan living guard, still clutching at the stump of his right arm, Selam heard shouts and screams from down below in the tavern's front room.

Word on what had happened up here was spreading. Soon, someone would come up to check what was going on and then -

Selam's thigh struck something hard, and he glanced down.

He had hit the side of the divan.

He looked back up to see Hafi's sword coming in again. Without thinking, Selam executed a spiraling parry that ended with Hafi's sword skittering across the floor off to the left and a bloody gash across his right cheek.

Hafi took a half-step back, his left hand rising to his cheek. He had a look of surprise on his face, like he had never conceived that such a thing could happen.

No less than Selam felt. He lowered his sword. "I'm sorry, brother. I - "

Hafi's sudden surge forward caught him unawares, and Selam froze again. This time for too long.

Hafi's hands clamped down around Selam's on the grip of the sword, and began twisting.

Selam was the stronger of the two of them. It had been thus for years. But now, this night, he found he could not resist the power of his brother's arms.

Slowly, inexorably, the point of Selam's sword moved. Twisting and rising until it was pointing upward between them.

Hafi grinned in sudden, made triumph.

Then he hurled himself onto the point of the sword.

It was like the world went into slow motion. Selam heard

himself cry out a denial, but it was from far away, in a distant country.

Hafi's body slid further down onto his blade, and he saw the pain in his brother's eyes. But also resolve.

And spite.

"What will you do now, my brother?" asked Hafi in a hoarse whisper.

Then his eyes glazed over, his breath rattled, and he went limp.

The world returned to normal speed and Selam pushed backwards, pulled the sword from his bother's body even as his mind screamed at him that this could not really be happening.

The door burst open to the side, and Selam heard Misra's voice.

"Fath - "

The youth broke off when he took in the scene. Selam turned to see his nephew's eyes grow wide with shock, then grief.

"Misra - " Selam began, then the youth's eyes met his, and grief turned to terrible anger.

Selam knew the young man would have a sword and be on him in a heartbeat. He also knew he could easily defeat Misra; he was good, but he had far too much still to learn.

But Selam had seen more than enough blood for one night. Precious blood that he never thought to spill.

He saw a second door off to the left, between a pair of tapestries that had been knocked askew.

He charged through it, then down the passage beyond toward the back of the tavern.

"Coward!" he heard Misra cry from behind him.

He found a set of stairs leading downward, and he followed them.

Selam was still running when dawn began to glimmer, bright and pure, in the sky to the west.

He had been running that direction ever since he emerged from the tavern's back door, ever since exiting one of Tyrash's half dozen gates, somehow getting there ahead of the news of the events at The Red Phoenix.

He ran until he had no strength left, but still he continued on.

Now, as the light of the new day bit into his eyes, eyes that could barely see from the tears still flowing from them, Selam finally slowed to a jog, then a walk.

Then he collapsed onto his knees and yelled. He yelled out the anger, the anguish of the night at that glowing orb that was slowly pushing its way up from where it had gone to bed a seeming lifetime ago.

He yelled until his throat was hoarse, then he sank down onto his haunches, and lowered his eyes.

The glint of steel drew his gaze, and he realized with a start that he was still carrying his father's sword, unsheathed in his right hand.

Sunlight glinted off the grey-blue of the curved, finely honed blade. Off the intricate engraving on the flat of the blade: game animals and constellations and weapons and men and horses all twisted into one mass of art that would have been garish, should have been garish, but somehow was instead sublime.

He looked at all that, and at the red stain of blood still coating the cutting edge in some places.

His brother's blood, along with others.

Selam raised his hand and drew back his arm, intending to just throw the sword away.

Except at the last second, the newly-dawned sunlight flashed against the pommel, the rounded metal that his father had made him trace with his fingertips countless times when he was a boy.

This was his family's legacy. His family's future.

Hafi had not seen that, not believed it. He had strayed from the path, and it had driven him, if not mad, at least to his end.

If Selam were to cast aside his legacy now, after all this. What would he be? And could he ever face his father without shame when they met again in the next world?

He lowered his arm again, letting the sword drop into the grass next to his knee, then he drew a deep breath.

Selam looked over his shoulder, to the east. Toward Tyrash, and the home he had always known.

He could never go back there. Maybe if he had not run, he could have explained. But running as he had...Misra would be past all convincing, and the authorities would have come to the same conclusion his nephew had: that Selam had killed his brother in cold blood.

Back was impossible. So it must be forward.

Selam looked back to the west, to the strange lands and unfamiliar kingdoms that lay toward the direction of the sunrise.

Then, slowly and deliberately, he cleaned the blood from his family's sword and sheathed it.

Then he rose, and took his first steps toward those distant lands.

HIDDEN MAGIC

A GLIMMER VALE CHRONICLES STORY

MICHAEL KINGSWOOD

AUTHOR OF *THE PERICLES CONSPIRACY*

HIDDEN MAGIC

On the run from the Magestirium, the keepers of the Kingdom's magical secrets, Melanie Klemins searches for a place a refuge, and perhaps even a home.

But peril lingers in even the most remote of cities, and the Magestirium has eyes everywhere.

Hidden Magic takes place before Glimmer Vale (Glimmer Vale Chronicles #1).

M elanie Klemins closed the door to her rooms and looked about carefully.

All appeared to be as she had left it, but she took her time, to be certain. She had seen so sign that the Inquisitors who were hunting her had arrived in Mangin City yet, but she couldn't afford to be wrong.

The sitting room was tidily arranged. A crimson-upholstered couch that was sized for two against the wall to her right, and a pair of similarly-upholstered chairs facing it across a darkly-stained low-cut table. A similarly-stained cabinet occupied the wall to the left, behind the chairs, where sat a white and red-striped porcelain tea set with settings for four, and a stoppered transparent decanter that was filled with a rich wine. A wrought-iron wood stove sat in the far right corner next to the couch, and the door to her sleeping chamber lay in the corner to her left as she came in.

Looking in the bed chamber, she saw her small four-poster bed, neatly made with blankets that matched the chairs' uphol-stery and carved from the same darkly-stained wood, night table, writing desk, and wardrobe. And, beneath the night table, the white porcelain chamber pot. And, most importantly, she saw the little scrap of paper she had left poking out of the desk, where its single drawer was slid shut and locked.

Melanie relaxed somewhat. At the least, no one had gone into her desk. She didn't fool herself that the lock would be particu-larly hard to get past; she could do it easily. But had someone done that, the odds of that little scrap being in the exact place she had left it before were slim.

Of course, that didn't mean someone hadn't been in here at all, and just not touched the desk.

She sniffed the air, but smelled only the lavender spray that the maids used when they came in to tidy up.

Melanie reached into the belt pouch on her right hip and pulled out a small paper package, filled with a carefully prepared and arranged collection of components. Her book of incantations was in a separate pouch, and she leafed through it until she found the correct one. The words and gestures were familiar to her, but she read them all the same before enacting the spell.

The component package flashed and crumpled into powder and smoke, the material of the components sacrificing themselves into the spell's energy.

The little flash expanded and swept through the room in a heartbeat, then was gone.

Melanie looked around again. If anyone had left a tracer or some other spell, or an item of some kind, in her rooms, it would show from a glow that only she could see. But there was nothing.

So. All was well.

Melanie sank down into the chair closest to the door leading out into the hallway, letting out a long breath, and allowed herself to relax. As much as was possible, anyway.

She had been going non-stop since fleeing the Capital. She changed methods of transport often: horseback to wagon to fancy carriage to riverboat and back to horseback, and hadn't dared to stay more than a few days in one place.

Too much risk of the Inquisitors catching up, and dragging her back like they had poor Timon.

Her heart wrenched as her last sight of him sprang back up into her mind. Beaten and bruised, mouth filled with a gag and bloody from a broken nose, but with a defiant stare for the Vigilant and his cronies who had him trussed up like a goose. That image, seen through the warped glass of the exterior window of their house, had brought her up short, terror and despair at their discovery halting her in her steps just as she was about to go in through their front door and be caught herself.

For an instant, she thought his eyes met hers through the glass, and they widened slightly. Then he gave the slightest of shakes of his head.

The Vigilant turned his head, and Melanie recognized him from the one time Timon had given in to her pleas and brought her into the Magestirium itself.

She didn't wait, she turned and ran. Fast as she could, she ran down the streets of the Capital to the storage house where Timon had stashed a getaway bag, for just such an occasion as this.

Then she took the next barge across the river to the mainland, and had begun her flight.

Now, months later in Mangin City, at the extreme northwest frontier of the Kingdom's domain, she thought maybe she might be able to stop running. She had been here a full day now, and so far during her examination of the city she had found no sign of pursuit or suspicion at all.

Maybe.

She looked down at herself, at the threadbare hem of her dress, the stains on her sleeves, the scuffs on her shoes, and decided she must look a sight. She was surprised she'd managed to get a room here at the Juggling Gypsy looking as she did. But, silver will overcome many an issue with appearances.

She leaned back into the cushions of her chair and considered.

Timon had stocked the getaway bag well. She had coin enough to last months, maybe years if she conserved it well. And though she had used up a fair amount of their store of components, she had enough to support a few more castings of the common incantations. But sooner or later she'd have to settle down someplace and find a way to make a living.

Perhaps -

A knock on the door jerked her upright in her chair, and her right hand went to the knife she kept on her left hip. She flexed the fingers of her left hand, feeling the comforting weight of the component bag tucked up her sleeve a way, and wished her heartbeat to silence so she could listen more closely to the goings on outside her door.

Another knock, then, "Mistress Klemins?"

Melanie recognized the Innkeeper's voice and relaxed. A bit. Standing, she moved over to the door and took hold of the latch. Then she took a quick breath and cracked the door open.

Oleg Kaversham was a heavyset man, with brown hair that had

mostly gone to grey and a matching beard, and only a beard: no mustache. Melanie had seen that look on other men before and always thought it ridiculous, but he managed to make it look almost dignified. He had the paunch that innkeepers always seemed to have, and wore the apron innkeepers always seemed to wear. But his apron was pristine, the white cloth not showing even the slightest smudge or stain. And his clothing beneath the apron was well-cut, from quality material. Not silk; that would be too ostentatious. But Melanie had known from her first look at him that his Inn did very good business, and he knew how to keep it that way.

Which was why she had opted to stay here, despite its ridiculous name.

Kaversham inclined his head slightly to her. "Good afternoon, Mistress Klemins. I located the store you inquired about." He held out a folded slip of paper, thrusting it into the gap between the door and jamb.

Melanie took the paper and returned the nod. "Thank you, Master Kaversham." She paused, then glanced down at herself again. And in that moment, she made her decision to stay a bit longer. "I think I will extend my stay."

Kaversham nodded. "For how long?"

She considered for a moment. "A week. Will that be acceptable?"

"Completely." In fact, he sounded quite a bit more pleased at the prospect than she would have expected. But then, it was early in the year, barely Spring yet. Fewer travelers braved the road in the winter.

Melanie decided not to make an issue of it.

"In that case, can you summon a seamstress please?"

Kaversham's right eyebrow tweaked upward ever so slightly, but he was wise enough to make no other comment. "I know just the lady. If I send my boy now, I believe she will likely arrive within the hour."

Which meant he had a contract with her shop, and probably

received a portion of the business he sent her way. A not unwise arrangement for an Innkeeper to have, especially one who ran a high-end establishment like his. Nor was it unusual. Well-to-do ladies often found the need for new clothing while traveling.

Still, Melanie always found the practice of not fully advertising the arrangement a tad underhanded.

Ah well, it was a small thing.

"Thank you," she said, and favored him with a smile. Then she shut the door.

The seamstress was prompt as the Innkeeper's word, and took Melanie's measurements with a practiced, professional air. She promised a three-day turnaround, and departed.

Though she was relatively at ease with the situation in the city and eager to seek out the store Kaversham had located for her, Melanie decided to remain in her rooms during those three days. She only came down for meals, and then she took a table in the rear of the common room, away from prying eyes.

Now that she was getting new attire, Melanie found herself much more self conscious about her state. The fewer people who saw her until she could get properly presentable, the better.

All the same, it was hard to wait. When the seamstress finally returned, Melanie had to restrain herself from either bouncing like a girl with giddiness or letting the seamstress have the rough side of her tongue, just because.

The dresses were pricey, but worth the coin, and the wait. Melanie left her rooms feeling renewed in a well-fitted dress of deep blue, with silver-white lace at the hem, cuffs, and neckline, and a matching cloak with a black-furred cowl for the lingering chill of the not-completely-departed winter.

A few heads turned as she passed through the common room of the Juggling Gypsy, and she couldn't help a warm feeling from the attention. She quickly suppressed that; she was on business. And besides, after Timon, she couldn't…

The heartache flared again and Melanie felt tears well up.

Foolish ninny. No time for this.

She paused near the door for a moment to collect herself. It took a moment, but when she stepped out into the sunlight of late morning, her head was high and she had herself under control again.

The Bowl And Quill was unlike any establishment Melanie had seen before.

Not so much because of the rows of shelves with attached wheeled ladders for access all the way to the top, or the seemingly endless number of tomes contained on those shelves, or the smell of dust and old paper. Those were the norm in a place like this.

No, what stood out about the place was its owner. He sat on a stool behind a counter that ran the length of the store at the rear, and he was made a sight.

His features were handsome enough, with strong cheekbones and a pronounced jaw, his broad shoulders speaking of physical strength that one would not expect from a man of bookish bent. But…

He wore rouge on a his cheeks. A lot of rouge. He clearly painted his lips as well; they were redder than nature would have made. His eyelids were colored a deep green that matched the irises of his eyes, and his golden locks flowed past his shoulders in plaited waves that looked as though a hairdresser had spent a week setting them just right.

Unlike Kaversham, he made no bones about garbing himself in bright blue silk. Not one to balk at ostentation was he.

Melanie liked him immediately.

The man looked her up and down as she approached the counter, though Melanie got the impression he was taking in the cut of her dress more than shape of her figure. His lips pursed ever so slightly and he rose from his stool.

"Good morning," he said, in a voice that was just a shade too high-pitched for as body as broad as his. "How may I serve you today?"

"You are the proprietor, I presume," Melanie said.

He nodded. "Hans Olbermon, at your service."

Melanie slipped her hand into the pouch she wore on her right hip, balancing out her belt knife. She withdrew a folded paper where she had written down the items she was looking for. "I'm told that in addition to books you also can procure more…specialized items." She held the paper out to him.

He took the paper and unfolded it. His eyebrows rose as he read, then his eyes flicked back to hers. His expression was one of carefully guarded curiosity. "Specialized, indeed. One does not often see an order such as this, except when members of the Magestirium come through town." His tone carried a hint of a question.

Melanie felt a little chill at his mention of the place, but she kept her face schooled to neutrality. "And have you received a similar order recently?"

A quick shake of his head. "Not in some months." He continued to stare at her for a long moment, and Melanie could feel the obvious question that he wanted to ask, and that she could not answer. But when it became plain she was not going to offer any further illumination he gave the slightest of shrugs and looked back down at the paper. "I have most of these," he said, "but the last two will take some time to acquire."

"How long?"

"A week, maybe two. Depends on my suppliers' schedules."

Melanie considered. That was longer than she had planned to stay at the Juggling Gypsy, but she suspected Oleg would not object to another extension. And it would be good to fully restock her store of components. There was no telling when she might get another chance; suppliers such as Hans were rare.

She nodded. "Very well. I will take what you have now. Send word to the Juggling Gypsy when the rest arrives."

"And to whom shall I send word?"

"Klemins. Melanie Klemins."

"One moment while I fill your order, Mistress Klemins."

She departed the Bowl and Quill with her new possessions carefully wrapped up into a nondescript paper bundle. There would be no reason for anyone to particularly want to make off with it, not from its appearance. But all the same, she kept it tucked in close to her body beneath her cloak as she threaded her way through the city's overcrowded streets to the Inn.

The relief she felt when she stepped inside was palpable. She hadn't realized how much her dwindling component inventory had been worrying her. But now with her stash mostly replenished, she felt a lot more ready to meet whatever came.

Oleg was behind the common room's bar when she came in, talking with a slender woman several years younger than he. She had thick black hair done up in a bun and was also wearing a white apron, though hers was stained and splotched in a number of places. Oleg noticed Melanie's entrance and gave a little nod in her direction, and the woman turned to follow his gaze.

She was beautiful. The kind of face that painters loved to recreate, with piercing blue eyes and a mouth that seemed made to smile.

"Mistress Klemins," Oleg said as she approached the bar, "I don't believe you've met my wife."

The woman smiled—she was definitely good at that—and said, "Sylive Kaversham, Mistress Klemins. I run the kitchens."

"You're the one I have to thank for those sweetmeats last night." The memory of that meal would have brought a smile to Melanie's lips even if Sylvie's pleasant demeanor hadn't already. "Very well done. You are a master of your craft."

Sylvie made a "posh" kind of sound and waved off Melanie's compliment, but she could tell the chef appreciated it.

Oleg grinned as well, but when he spoke, he was all business. "Anything we can do for you, Mistress Klemins?"

Melanie paused, considering. As the days had passed with no sign of pursuit or even awareness of a fugitive on the run, she was becoming more comfortable here. Today's excursion had confirmed what she had begun to suspect: this might be a place where she could settle. Finally.

"Do you know of any rooms for let?"

Oleg exchanged looks with his wife, their expressions clouding, and Melanie realized she may have given the impression she was dissatisfied with their service. She hurried to clarify.

"I have been traveling for a long time, and I feel the need to settle down. It strikes me that Mangin City may be the place for it."

Relief flashed across their faces, and Oleg nodded. "I have seen a few advertisements, but none that you would likely find appealing. Rougher neighborhoods, you understand. But I will put out some inquiries."

"Thank you."

The sun had sunk down below the buildings in the east and the sky had gone a deep crimson as Melanie made her way back toward the Juggling Gypsy.

She had spent the last two days examining a number of available flats from a list Oleg had procured for her. Most were unimpressive, but this last she had come from was, she was sure, the one. Half of the top floor of a four story building overlooking the city's main square, it was exactly the place for her. Close to many different businesses where she could potentially earn some coin, at the center of entertainments in the city, but above the milling, stinking mob.

In other words, it was perfect.

She had a spring in her step as she slipped through the

crowded streets, and was riding high on a wave of excited euphoria as she considered this new chapter that was about to open in her life.

But as she rounded a corner onto the Inn's street, she came to an abrupt halt. The crowd, and the wagons and carriages, were at a standstill. She was tall, but not tall enough to see past the group of men in front of her to spot what was going on. So she tugged at one man's cloak.

He scowled back at her.

"What's going on?"

He shrugged. "Fool ran his wagon into a carriage and the carriage flipped. Street's blocked."

Melanie felt her good cheer fading into annoyance. The Inn was just a block down, but she might as well be on the other side of the Kingdom.

She cast about and saw a narrow gap between two buildings off to the right. That alley, unless she missed her guess, meandered behind the Juggling Gypsy and its neighboring buildings, and would rejoin the street somewhere ahead. She could get past this obstruction and save a lot of time, using it.

The shadows were long, and the interior of the alley was darkening quickly as sunset faded into twilight, but it shouldn't take more than a few minutes. And she had her knife and a full pouch of components.

She went for it.

It was darker than it had looked from out on the street, but also surprisingly clean. When she reached the back of the building and turned into the alley proper, she saw why. Rather than simply throwing rubbish out the windows, the citizens of the city had created receptacles for their waste and trash, closed bins that stood next to the rear doors of the buildings on either side of the alley. And the alley itself was broad enough that a small wagon could be driven down it; Melanie suspected the city periodically had workers come through to remove the refuse.

Not a bad scheme, that.

She turned left and hurried onward, eager to get clear of the alley despite its relative cleanliness.

It did not run in a straight line, instead meandering its way around the backs of the buildings, some of which extended further back from the street than others.

She came up on a larger building that she thought was the Juggling Gypsy from the slant of its roof and the construction of what window panes were visible from back here, and turned to the right. Up ahead, the alley snaked left as it reached the rear of the building.

For a moment, the turn to the left brightened, then just as quickly the light winked out and Melanie heard the faint sound of a door shutting. Someone had either come out into the alley or gone inside.

A shriek rang out. A woman's yell, followed by a man's curse. No, two men.

Melanie froze, uncertainty causing her to fumble about for what to do.

Then the woman cried out again, and that sound unlocked the hold on Melanie's mind. She surged forward, her hand dipping into her component pouch.

She kept most of her incantations written down into a book; they were too complicated to commit fully to memory and the consequences of doing them incorrectly were dire enough that only a fool would risk it. But Timon had insisted she memorize a few simpler ones, for self defense purposes.

Melanie racked her brain for the incantation for force as she rushed toward the bend in the alley, silently praying she didn't do it wrong.

The scene before her when she rounded the corner was terrifying, but none too unexpected or unusual. A pair of men in roughly-made, threadbare clothes, barely more than rags, were holding a struggling apron-clad woman between the two of them, while a third was searching through a pile of rubbish from an upended bag that lay thrown on the ground off to the side.

Melanie figured it out in a rush. The woman had been taking the refuse out. These fellows were either rooting through the leavings in the alley or were waiting for some poor soul to come out, and they'd jumped her.

Well. That was a poor move on their part.

"This all you got in here?" the scrounging man said, sounding disgusted. "From that fancy Inn?"

Melanie drew herself up and pulled the little packet of components out, clenching it in her right hand. Then she said, loudly, "Release her."

The trio of men stopped, as did the woman, and all eyes turned toward Melanie. The men were nameless dreks, but the woman -

Melanie recognized Sylvie, and it sent a shock through her system, bringing her up short from surprise.

That almost cost her dearly.

"You look like you've got some coin," the man who had been pawing through the refuse said. "Give it up." And he launched himself toward her. His hands came down on her shoulders and she stumbled backward.

She would have fallen over, but his leap carried him at an angle, so she struck the wall instead. He wasn't so lucky. When she struck, his momentum carried him past her to the right, and he rebounded off the wall and stumbled to the ground.

He quickly began to right himself, though, his eyes burning with embarrassed anger.

Melanie's mind sprang back into action, and she slid away from him, raising her hands in front of herself. The words of the force incantation flew from her mouth so quickly and easily it was like someone else was voicing them, and she traced the gestures out that would combine the words and the component's destruction into effect.

The component packet dissolved into dust and smoke, and she felt the energy of the spell flowing into her.

She pushed, and the man was hurled backwards, his eyes widening in shock.

He struck the far wall and slid down, stunned.

Melanie turned toward Sylvie and the other two men, and all three mouths were agape.

The man to Sylvie's left recovered first. He released her arm and pulled a pathetically rusted knife from behind his back, where he had it tucked in his belt, no doubt. But though it was obviously not well-kept, Melanie had no illusions it could do its job if she let him.

She didn't.

The spell was still functioning, and he could no more resist the force she gripped him with than a boat can resist the waves of a storm. She pulled him forward, and he went careening head-first into the door at the back of the Inn. He bounced off and fell to the ground, immobile.

That left the one remaining. Melanie turned away from the man fallen before the door and focused on him.

His eyes were wide with fright now. He grabbed Sylvie by both arms and tried to position himself behind her, using her to shield himself from Melanie's attack.

Instead, Sylvie brought her heel down hard on the arch of his foot.

The man howled and released her. She stumbled forward just as Melanie heard the Inn door slam open.

"What's goes on here!" came a masculine roar at the same time Melanie thrust with force again.

The final thug tried to raise his hands against the invisible attack, but he too was flung backwards into the wall.

Off to the right, the first attacker had regained his feet. He swayed, looking from his companions to Melanie to something behind her. He swallowed, then said, "You'll pay for this, witch. Magestirium will see you hang!"

Then he turned and sprinted around the corner, fast as his feet could carry him.

Melanie lowered her hands and looked behind her.

Oleg was there, holding the obviously shaken Sylvie as she clung to him. They both looked at Melanie with expressions that mixed anger, relief, gratitude, fear, and confusion all at once.

Melanie had never been in the kitchens of the Juggling Gypsy before, but they were smaller than she would have expected. A single long wooden table, chairless, dominated the center of the room. A great stone fireplace for baking lay along the alley-side of the room, and large steel bowls on pivots hung over a second fire pit on the right-hand wall. The left side held cabinets that no doubt held the tools of the trade, and several bins for ingredients. Another, smaller, table sat near the double doors to the common room, surrounded by a quartet of chairs.

Sylvie sat in one of the chairs, facing Melanie, who stood with her back to the closed door leading back into the alley. Oleg was tending a cut on her forehead that Melanie hadn't noticed before during all the excitement.

No one had said anything for quite a while. Oleg had simply led Sylvie inside and began seeing to her injury, and Melanie had followed. Now, Sylvie was looking at her with that same partly confused expression, and Oleg wasn't looking at her at all, focusing instead on his wife.

When it seemed the tension had grown so one could cut it with a knife, Sylvie finally broke the silence.

"How is it that you—a woman—can work magic? That is forbidden. The Magestirium don't allow it."

There it was. The thing Melanie had been running from, even as she embraced it. Now that it was out there, she waited in silence, hands clenched together in front of her. The condemnation would come now.

Instead, Oleg snorted. "Magestirium. I ran into some of their people in my Navy days. Their spells are impressive but they're pompous windbags, the lot of them." He finally looked away from the rag he was holding onto Sylvie's forehead and at Melanie. There was no condemnation there.

Nor was there judgment in Sylvie's eyes.

Melanie looked away from the two of them, unsure how or where to begin explaining. Finally, she shrugged. "Not all of them are like that. There was one…Timon…" Saying his name brought the pain up again, but she forced it down. Drawing a breath, she said, "I was working in the Capital, and met him at the midwinter festival. We walked out for a time, and then things grew more serious between us. I grew more and more interested in what he did. At first he would not speak of it, but…" She shrugged. "We fell in love, and he taught me in secret."

"What happened?" Sylvie asked.

Melanie shuddered. "Somehow they found out, and the Inquisitors came for us. I saw them take him….and I ran." She closed her eyes, and saw that scene of Timon, tied and beaten but undefeated again. "I've been running ever since."

"Well." Oleg's words drove the image from Melanie's mind, and she opened her eyes to look at him. He had stood and was looking toward the swinging doors to his common room. After a second, he drew breath and said, "I wouldn't turn you over to likes of the Magestirium even if you hadn't helped Sylvie." He turned and looked back at Melanie, and there was firm resolve in his eyes. "Your secret's safe with us."

In her chair, Sylvie nodded agreement.

"But," Oleg pointed back toward the alley, "can't say the same for that lot. They'll tell their friends, and word will spread there's a woman in Mangin City working magic. That'll get back to the Magestirium sure as thunder follows lightning."

Melanie nodded, a sinking feeling coming into her belly. "I can't stay here."

Oleg shook his head. "No, I think not. You're here when they come, they're going to find you. If you're not, and they find nothing, they'll write it off as sour grapes, or someone trying to put a frame on an herb woman. Then it dies."

"It might not," Sylvie interjected. "They won't want to admit they were bested by a woman. Might not say anything, or if they do they'll say you chased them away." She smiled up at her husband. "Which you were about to do."

Oleg looked doubtful, but mulled it over.

Melanie beat him to it, shaking her head. "You may be right, Sylvie. But I can't risk it. If I stay here it'll be nothing but looking over my shoulder forever." She pushed the despair, the anger down. She had finally found a place that might be safe to settle in, and that hope was dashed. It took all her effort not to break down. But she could not. Instead, she drew a deep breath and said, "I'll check out tomorrow morning. Is there someplace I can buy a horse?"

Oleg and Sylvie shared a look. "There'll be no charge for the room." He held up a hand to forestall Melanie's protest. "Your help today was payment enough. As for the horse," he gestured to the north, "try the warehouse section near the north gate. They've got stables. You can probably get a horse there. Might find a caravan to travel with as well. It's safer than going alone."

Melanie nodded. That wasn't a bad idea. "I'll do that, then." She began toward the door to the common room, but stopped after a couple paces. She looked back at them. "I have a delivery scheduled from the Bowl And Quill. Some items that are very difficult to find. I'm unsure where else I can obtain them."

Sylvie nodded. "Leave us the coin for it, and we'll keep it for you. Whenever you get where you're going, send us a pigeon and we'll forward it along." She paused, the added, "And if you come back this way again, please come and see us again."

That was a genuine offer; her eyes showed that plainly. Glancing at Oleg again, Melanie could tell he shared the sentiment. That helped melt part of the icicle of despair that had been threatening to pierce her heart.

She nodded, putting on a smile for them. "Thank you."

The warehouse section was even more busy than the rest of Mangin City. But its business was more controlled, almost a choreographed interplay of supply and demand, coming and going. If she didn't know better, Melanie would have thought there was some great invisible hand guiding it all.

There was not, of course. It was just people doing what they do. But at least here, they were all about more or less the same purpose.

Oleg was right, there were several stables, and Melanie contemplated going in and picking out a horse for herself. But in the square inside the north gate, she saw a group of half a dozen wagons and fifteen or twenty men apparently getting ready to depart. Men were tying down straps on boxes of goods. Others who were obviously hired swords in the role of caravan guard were inspecting their mounts and doing a last check of their gear.

And one man, dressed nicer than the rest, though by no means opulently, stood off to the side, reviewing a document that was attached to a wooden board and occasionally checking off some item or other with a piece of charcoal.

Melanie approached him and stopped a pace away. It took him a while to notice, caught up in his paperwork as he was. But eventually he glanced up and saw her.

An eyebrow rose, and he lowered his document. "Can I help you, my lady?"

Melanie almost corrected the term of address, but stopped herself. If he took her for a noblewoman, so much the better. "Are you the master of this caravan?" She gestured toward the cluster of wagons and men.

He nodded. "Sure am. Samel Tersol," he said, introducing himself.

"Where are you bound and when do you depart?"

Samel snorted. "We depart as soon as I complete my last tally."

He shook his document slightly. "We head to Calas, by way of Glimmer Vale."

Melanie had heard of Calas. It was one of the Kingdom's holdings west of the Saddleback Mountains, and the staging area for the war effort against the Hermelite Empire. But the other?

"Glimmer Vale?"

Samel chuckled. "Not many people know it. Little valley in the western half of the Saddleback Mountains. There's a town there, Lydelton, and a some farmsteads. They do a lot of fishing in the lake." He shrugged. "It's a nice enough place, but there's not much to it." He looked sidelong at her. "Why do you ask?"

"Do you have room for passengers? I can pay."

He blinked, looking taken aback. "Passengers? I suppose but," he trailed off, then shook his head. "Begging your pardon my lady, but why would a lady like you want to travel with us? You seem more the carriage type."

Melanie drew herself up. "That is my business. Do you have room or not?"

"Sure."

"And how long is the journey?"

Samel did a quick tally in his head. "Normally I'd say three weeks to Glimmer Vale, but this time of year there's still snow in some of the passes so probably a month. Stop a few days in Lydelton to resupply and do some trading, then it's another couple weeks to Calas. So, say two months total, to be safe."

She nodded. That sounded perfect. "Very well, Master Tersol. Will I need my own horse or do you have room in a wagon?"

He shrugged. "Up to you."

They exchanged coin, and Melanie took a seat next to the driver of the third wagon in the caravan after setting her belongings in the bed behind her.

As they set out, Melanie looked back at Mangin City, and again felt a pang in her heart. She hadn't dared to think any of the places she had traveled through could end up being home before.

Allowing herself to do so here, and having it turn out so poorly… She despaired of ever finding a place again.

That was nonsense, of course, and she shook herself out of that melancholy train of thought. Instead, she turned back to looking ahead, to the mountain pass, to Glimmer Vale, and then Calas beyond.

And maybe, some day, to a home.

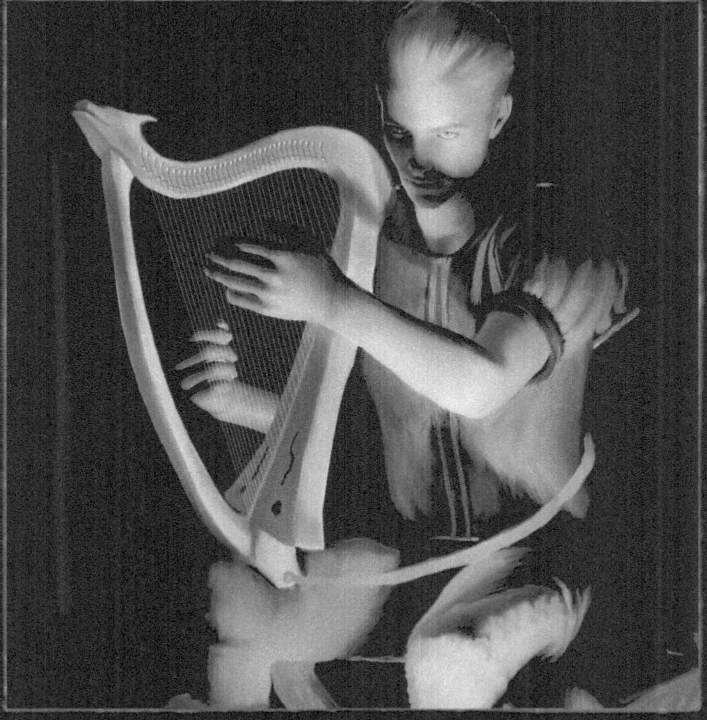

CAPTIVE HEARTS
A GLIMMER VALE CHRONICLES STORY
MICHAEL KINGSWOOD
AUTHOR OF THE PERICLES CONSPIRACY

CAPTIVE HEARTS

Hamel lingers in Mangin City, performing in taverns for board as he searches for a way to rescue his imprisoned brother.

But the city is full of intrigues, some dangerous enough to overcome even the wit and skill of a trained Bard such as he.

Captive Hearts takes place between Out-Dweller (Glimmer Vale Chronicles #2) and Tollard's Peak (Glimmer Vale Chronicles #3).

Hamel took a long draw from his tankard. He felt the foam soak his mustache as he downed three swallows of The Juggling Gypsy's house ale, and savored the subtle flavor of the hops the brewer had used.

That was good stuff.

He bent over on his stool and lowered the tankard to the polished pine planks of the stage that dominated the common room opposite the bar and straightened, then took a moment to look out at the evening's crowd.

The room was about three-quarters full tonight, the long tables and benches surrounding the stage filled with a wide assortment of people. Traveling merchants in their finely-crafted wools and the occasional silk and their muscle-bound guards who even here always seemed to have a dagger or two close to hand. More roughly-dressed laborers who lived and worked in the blocks surrounding the Inn. The black-bearded blacksmith's apprentice from down the street and a gushing and extremely well-proportioned blonde who could only be his special girl. A handful of men who, from their haircuts and how they seemed to constantly be sizing the situation up even while at their ease, Hamel presumed were off-duty members of the city watch.

Further back in one of the booths sat a fancily-dressed couple that could have been from a minor noble house from the cut of their clothes and the obvious gold on the woman's neck.

Another booth in the rear corner held a trio of darker men in cowled cloaks, who had barely budged from their table all night while they nursed their drinks.

People from all walks of life had come to hear him play, and give him their coin.

With a little thrown in for Oleg, the innkeeper, as well, of course.

It was hot, and not just because of the lamplight being focused on him from sconces lining the base of the stage. The sun was only just now beginning to set despite the late hour, and the lingering heat of the mid-summer day had only just begun to dissipate. His back was soaked with sweat, and his armpits as well, making his bright blue shirt stick to his torso.

It was more than enough to require him to wet his whistle, even if he hadn't been singing for most of the last hour. But he couldn't tarry for long; the audience always wanted more and his set was not yet finished.

He adjusted himself on his chair, lifted his harp into position on his left knee, and grinned at the crowd.

"Requests?" he said.

Almost immediately came a call for "Maiden's Kiss" from one of the off-duty watchmen. Hamel suppressed an inward groan; someone always wanted to hear that one. But he'd long ago learned to give the audience what they want…and then just a little more, if he wanted to keep the coin flowing.

Hamel inclined his head toward the guardsman, then gave a quick strum of his harp.

After a second's pause he began picking out the introductory chord progression, a cheerful jaunt in C Major, and began tapping out the beat with his right foot.

After a few bars, the audience on the benches picked up the beat and began to keep it themselves, rapping their knuckles or their tankards on the tables. Once they had it, Hamel stopped his tapping and began to sing.

"My maiden fair, she sits right there

And oh what a lucky lad am I.

She waits for me, with eyes like the sea

And a smile that would brighten the sky."

As he progressed through the first verse, he felt the energy of the song grow, reflected and enhanced by the crowd as those who knew the words tried to join in. The tips of his fingers began to tingle where they contacted the strings of his harp, and the energy coursed up his arms and into his torso. The tingling sensation spread through the rest of his body until he felt like his hair was standing on end.

And onward he sang, into the second verse.

The lyrics flowed out as though driven by a force of their own and he was merely a conduit. But a conduit with will.

He swept his gaze across the audience again, his practiced eye assessing them at a glance. He shifted the tenor of his voice slightly, and the song's energy responded to him, flowing from his harp through his fingers and then out from his voice, and to the audience's ears. The infusions of intent he gave from the tonal shift had an immediate effect, to his trained eye.

All around the room, the customers perked up, their cares visibly sliding away as the magic of his music infused them. They sat straighter, smiled broader, and the couples looked at each other more fondly.

He couldn't have stopped if he wanted to. The currents of the music, and the magic it wove, carried him with it until he reached the last stanza.

"My maiden fair, she kissed me right there!"

A full bar's rest. Then,

"And oh what a lucky lad am I."

A final strum of his harp, and the audience erupted into a mix of joyous laughter and applause. Those on the benches and tables nearest the stage pounded their tankards on the tabletop appreciatively.

The applause continued and Hamel soaked it up.

This was what he lived for.

As he made a quick bow from the waist, he noticed the cowled men departing through the Inn's front door. Then the crowd renewed their shouts of approval, and he cast the men from his mind.

The Inn was closing up.

The last of the customers were finishing their drinks beneath the stern eyes of Oleg's two bouncers, big fellows in grey tabards who Hamel heard were newly back from the war. Must have got out before the Crown decreed a moratorium on releases from enlistment. Lucky bastards.

The bouncers chivvied the drunks on to greater speed as Oleg's three barmaids—two bright and spritely lasses just off their mothers' purse strings and one older woman who could have been a grandmother and who watched the others like a hawk, warding off untoward behavior from the customers before the bouncers even knew it was beginning—moved through the common room, pushing brooms to clear up the night's detritus.

Hamel rubbed his cleaning rag over the arms of his harp and gently set it into its carrying case. The case was finely constructed of polished blackwood that was closed and locked by a pair of silver clasps. But it paled in comparison to the beauty and workmanship of the instrument itself.

Morelli himself had crafted it. Carved the arms from an ancient oak that had been struck down in a lightning storm, and stained it until it was nearly golden in hue. Hamel had played many a harp, but none matched this one for tone and comfort of play.

It was his most prized possession.

Across the bar from where he sat, Oleg poured him another tankard and plopped it down onto the counter.

"Good night tonight," the Innkeeper said as Hamel took another swig. He had brown hair that was going to grey and was bearded, but without a mustache. His belly pressed against the immaculate white of the apron he always wore. But there was muscle below that fat, and the ability to use it.

Hamel had never had any illusions about that.

"Aye," said Hamel, and grinned at him. "Did you expect anything else?"

Oleg chuckled and shook his head. "Not when you are here, my friend." He turned and walked down to the end of the bar nearest the swinging doors leading to the kitchen, where Sylvie, the Inn's head chef and Oleg's wife, had their strongbox open and was doing a count of the night's take.

She was a bit too old for Hamel's taste, though decidedly younger than Oleg and still attractive, with black hair done up in a bun and a warm, friendly smile. Her apron was never pristine; the zest with which she practiced her trade was plain to see from the stains and spots where the kitchen pots and nipped at her.

The couple conferred for a few minutes and three more swigs of ale, then she passed a pouch to Oleg. He bounced it and raised an eyebrow at her. Only after she nodded assent did he return and drop the pouch down on the countertop next to Hamel's tankard.

Hamel eyed the pouch. It was standard sized, but it bulged.

Picking it up, he loosened the drawstrings and looked within.

It was all silver, or near enough to it. A very good night indeed.

Looking from his pay back at Oleg, he grinned, then swallowed the rest of his ale in a long series of gulps. Then he stood from his barstool, slung his harp case over his left shoulder, and tied the pouch of coins to his belt.

"Why do you never take a room when you play here?" Oleg asked.

Hamel grinned at him. "And deprive my lady-friends of all this?" he said, spreading his arms wide in a stance that shouted, "Look over here".

Oleg shook his head and rolled his eyes, but he could not hold back a chuckle. "Good night, Hamel," he said.

"Night."

Hamel strode past the barmaids as they attended to their cleaning duties, then out into the streets of Mangin City.

He paused for a few seconds as the Inn's door latched shut behind him and breathed in the night air. Overhead, a crescent moon amidst the endless multitude of stars cast a dim illumination that seemed to only lengthen the shadows of the city streets. Mostly devoid of traffic at this hour, the streets seemed almost peaceful, and the normal stink of bodies and manure and rubbish had faded a bit. The air had lost its summer oppression, becoming pleasantly cool.

Hamel soaked it all in and breathed out a contented breath, then pushed his contentment aside as he truly got about the night's business.

He turned left toward the more heavily traveled thoroughfares and then to the South side, where he had rented a short-term flat not far from the city's jailhouse and the law court.

He needed to take another look around the jail. Though Hamel was pretty sure he'd figured out where his brother Theobald's cell was located, a means of ingress still alluded him. If he -

His musing was interrupted when a pair of figures stepped out from the shadows on either side of the street in front of him and blocked his path. Broad-shouldered men in cowled cloaks they were, and they carried themselves like they knew how to take care of business.

The sound of more movement from behind, and Hamel turned his head slightly so he could look back.

Another man, big and cowled, had appeared at his back, his arms hanging at his sides in a way that someone who didn't know what to look for would think was a stance of complete relaxation.

He was the most dangerous of the bunch.

"Minstrel," one of the men to his front said, and Hamel ground his teeth at the insult. He looked at the speaker.

The man had stepped a pace forward, and the angle of his head in the moonlight allowed a smidgeon of his face to come into view. Hamel suddenly remembered him from within the Juggling Gypsy, and cursed himself for not paying greater attention to him and his companions earlier.

"My lord wishes to meet with you," the man continued.

Before Hamel could ask who his lord was, the clop clop of hoofbeats made him look behind himself again.

A two-horse carriage came out of the gloom, driven by a fourth cloaked man, and pulled up alongside Hamel on his right. It was darkly-painted, sized for four, with paned windows and a latching door on the side closest to him.

And on the upper-left corner of the passenger compartment

where it would easily be seen by onlookers, Hamel could just make out a coat of arms: a rearing lion overtop a stylized shield, with crossed saber and spear. The coat of arms of House Mineus, the second wealthiest of the noble houses in this region of the Kingdom.

A moment before, Hamel thought he was about to have to fight off robbers, or murderers. That would have been dangerous, but doable; nothing he hadn't seen to before a dozen times over. But seeing that crest, he wished it had only been hoodlums who had accosted him tonight.

He had to stop himself from groaning. It wouldn't do to let these hirelings see his sudden fright.

"Alright," he said. "Let's go."

The carriage had seats for four, so naturally the three cowled men got in with Hamel. Almost as if they didn't trust him, or something.

As soon as the door latched, the driver got the horses moving, and they set off. Hamel settled back into the admittedly well-stuffed cushions of his seat for a long ride, but found himself surprised when instead of turning toward the west gate, which was the closest to the Mineus estates, they turned to the left, toward Mangin City's central square.

It was to be the Lord's town house then. Interesting.

Only a few minutes passed before they came to a halt and Hamel's escorts opened the door and disembarked. They waited while he took his time in exiting; no need to show his nerves by rushing to their every beck and call.

The town house was three stories tall, and separated from its neighbors, also owned by nobility or very wealthy trading families, by a wrought-iron fence with sharp points at its top. The courtyard where the carriage had stopped was little more than a half-circle of paving stones before the steps leading to the house's front door, and separated from the street by a gate that a pair of servants were just now rushing to close.

As far as town houses went, it was plain. None of the ornate engravings and gargoyles that Hamel has seen on other, usually less highly ranked, family houses. To his mind, that just made the immense wealth of the owner all that much more obvious.

The hireling who had spoken on the streets said, "This way," and took the lead, mounting the steps to the house's double front doors. A servant that Hamel hadn't noticed in his first glance around, plainly adorned in blue livery with the house's coat of arms on his left breast, stepped over and opened the door before the hireling had finished ascending, and kept it open while Hamel and the rest of his entourage followed.

The interior of the house continued the trend its exterior had started: simple, reserved decor that almost approached spare but to a trained eye screamed opulence. But more than that, opulence coupled with self-discipline and taste.

Hamel had heard Lord Mineus was not one to be trifled with. Without having even seen the man, he decided those rumors were true.

He would have to be cautious here.

The hireling led Hamel up a stairwell that was covered in a thick blue rug that ran its entire width and length in one meticu-lously-woven piece, then down a short hallway to a trio of darkly-stained oak doors: one at the end of the hall and two others facing each other a few feet before the first.

Stopping before the door at the end of the hall, the hireling turned around and faced Hamel, his arms crossed over his chest and his feet planted like it would take a giant to move him.

Hamel slowed, unsure what this meant, and stopped between the two other doors. One of the two remaining hirelings, who had been trailing, took up station to Hamel's right, blocking access to that door, and he understood.

There was only one way the Lord wanted him to go, and several places he desired remain sacrosanct.

Hamel turned to his left to the last door, and the last remaining hireling, the one who had stood so menacingly still on the street, knocked, then pushed it open, gesturing or Hamel to follow him.

Past the door was another vista of simple elegance. A sitting room, with one long blue-upholstered couch and two single-person chairs set up in a loose circle around a fireplace in the left-hand wall that appeared made of hewn marble. The wall opposite the door Hamel came through was dominated by a trio of bookshelves that were filled with tomes thin and thick. A quick sweep of his gaze across their spines showed histories, biographies, dissertations on philosophy and natural law. All the things a well brought-up man of means and power should know of.

A small fire flickered in the fireplace, lending a cheerful light to the room that accentuated that from the oil lamps on the walls and added the faint odor of pine smoke.

Combined with the broad cabinet along the right wall that held bottles of vintages that Hamel knew to range from rare to almost un-findable, it was a very pleasant room, indeed.

A man was sitting in one of the single-person chairs near the fireplace. He was getting past his middle years, with black hair that was fighting a losing battle against grey and a mustache that had already lost. He wore a well-cut red jacket that appeared made from the finest wool, and was held closed by buttons that reflected the firelight so that at first Hamel thought they were made of gold. But when the man moved to place the book he had been reading down on the little table between the chair and the couch, Hamel saw they were merely silver.

Merely.

The man's leggings were grey, and cut loose in the current fashion, and he had a golden signet ring capped with a not insubstantial ruby on the ring finger of his right hand.

Lod Mineus, Hamel presumed.

The hireling snapped his heels together and brought himself erect before making a quick but respectful bow. Gesturing toward

Hamel, he said, "The minstrel, as you ordered my lord," in an emotionless, gravely voice.

Again with the minstrel. Hamel cast baleful eyes on the hireling for a moment before looking back at the nobleman.

Mineus had risen form his chair. He gave Hamel a quick once-over with his eyes, then shook his head and made a soft tsk-ing sound as he turned his attention back to the hireling. "Come now, Rubert. Master Isenholf is no mere minstrel wandering from town to town playing for scraps and trifles. He is a graduate of the Morested Academy. Bard would be the appropriate title." He raised his left eyebrow and looked back at Hamel. "Would it not?"

Hamel froze.

His mind went completely blank from shock for a second as the import of the lord's words hit him like a sledgehammer.

How in the hell did he know all that?

Hamel never gave anyone his surname, especially now after Theo's very public disgrace. And as for the rest...

The older man's gaze remained on him, seeming to see right through to his core. Hamel gave himself an inward shake. This was no time to be off his game.

He made an inclination of his head toward Mineus. It should have been a full bow, but the Academy's pedigree made the gesture acceptable, if only just barely.

"It is, my lord." He felt unduly proud that he managed to keep his voice steady.

Mineus' lips turned slightly upwards, saying without words that he knew every question that was running through Hamel's head right then.

The nobleman held his gaze for a second longer, then turned and walked across the room to the wine cabinet. As he walked, he spoke again. "You first came to my attention some months ago, when you last were in Mangin City. I was most taken by your rendition of Locrati's Mia Volunta." A crystal decanter atop the cabinet was filled with a purplish-red liquid. Mineus lifted it and poured out a portion into two glasses that were resting next to the decanter. Replacing the decanter atop the cabinet, he took up the glasses and turned back to Hamel.

"I had my men, and some of my contacts down south, look into you, and it struck me you are a man whose talents might be useful someday." He held out one of the glasses to Hamel, and his smile broadened. "That day is today."

Hamel accepted the glass and looked down into the liquid. Purple-red, devoid of blemish or sediment. He gave the glass a quick swirl, sending the fluid spinning ever so slowly around the interior, and sniffed.

A hint of plum. A bit of spice.

Very nice.

He raised the glass to his mouth and sipped, then swished the wine around to fully absorb the flavor. It was every bit as excellent as the nose advertised.

Swallowing, he raised the glass again, in salute to Mineus. "Excellent vintage. Thank you, my lord."

Mineus inclined his head ever so slightly; an unschooled man would not have even noticed it. Then he, too, took a drink.

They stood there in silence for a time. Mineus no doubt expected Hamel to take the bait and ask how exactly he thought Hamel could be useful to him. And he probably should. But Hamel was still feeling off center from the nobleman's revelation of knowledge.

Better to let him volunteer it than risk giving anything more away.

Another couple seconds passed, and then Mineus broke. He let out an almost chuckle and turned away from Hamel. As he walked back toward the fireplace, he said, "You have, no doubt, heard of Lord Bortimar's recent tragedy."

Hamel nodded. "I have."

Everyone had; it was the talk of the town. The news had come back to Mangin City from Calas just three days ago. Lord Bortimar's son and heir, Geofram, had been killed in battle while leading his Company against the Hermelite Empire. His sacrifice ensured the survival of an entire Division of the Kingdom's troops. But despite that great honor, it was a tragedy that had struck the aging lord to his core.

Mineus placed one hand on the mantel above the fireplace and looked down into the flames. "Poor Lord Bortimar is now left without an heir, only his young daughter Lucilla." He shook his head sadly.

It was mock sadness, Hamel was certain. After only a few minutes with the Lord, he was beginning to read him a bit. And Lord Mineus was not as broken up about this turn of events as he wanted to put on.

"She is a comely girl, and recently flowered." Mineus sipped from his glass and looked back at Hamel, that left eyebrow rising again. "It happens my son Stepan has just reached his ascendancy. Lord Bortimar and I are old friends," which meant that Mineus and he had long been rivals sparring against each other for power, position, and wealth, "and I would hate to see his estate divided by the crown for lack of a valid heir." He smiled at Hamel then, and Hamel got a little shiver down his spine.

"As you know, two days from now is the seventy-fifth anniversary of the founding of the Royal Marshalls. In their honor, I am having a ball. Lord Bortimar and his daughter will be in attendance." He turned fully away from the fire and sipped at his wine again. "During that ball, I would like you to work some of your Bardic magic, to help bring about the joining of our two families."

Hamel had just been lifting his glass to his lips when Mineus said this. He about choked.

Moving quickly to avoid spilling any of the precious fluid, he lowered the glass and pressed his free hand to his mouth. He had to work for a second to swallow his mouthful instead of spewing it out all over the Lord's floor.

All the while, his mind flashed with the need to run, panic threatening to make him do so as he looked from the Lord to his hireling. Mineus had just revealed something that -

He got himself under control again and shook his head vigor-ously. "My Lord, I only play music and recite ballads, I - "

"Don't play coy with me, boy." All hint of congeniality was gone, the Lord's tone gone to stone as he thrust his right index finger at Hamel. "I know well the Academy's curriculum, and of its sanction from the Magestirium."

By the Gods.

Hamel looked back at the hireling, who stood there implacable as a statue. Mineus could not just talk about this in front of someone not of the landed nobility!

"My lord," Hamel began, but the nobleman cut him off, his tone lessened in its harshness as Mineus apparently came to understand the reason for Hamel's dissemblance.

"You needn't worry about Rubert, Master Isenholf. He has kept my secrets for fifteen years. I assure you, yours, and those of your Academy, will be just as sacrosanct as mine."

Easy for him to say. He didn't stand to have the penalty of sanguinity imposed on him if he revealed what had to be hidden.

But looking at the aging Lord, and the determined expression on his face, he knew there was no point in denial. As well, Hamel had the strong suspicion the hireling would make it extremely unpleasant if the Lord decided he needed to, and despite his earlier confidence on the street, having observed Rubert more closely for a time now, Hamel decided there was no way he could stop him.

Sighing, Hamel lowered his eyes and nodded slowly. "How did you learn of it?"

Mineus snorted. "I led a battalion in the Tyrashi campaign twenty-five years ago. Do you think I didn't know what the Bards under my command were capable of, or what they did?"

That made sense. Hamel took another drink, this one much longer. Then he shook his head. "Alright. But what you ask is..." He trailed off, then looked back up at the Lord. "Our magic is a subtle one, and limited. That's why the Magestirium allows us our independence. I can affect moods and morale, and that's about it. I can't make someone fall in love."

"Love." Mineus snorted. "Who said anything about love? I happen to know my son has some affection for Lucilla, and she for him. But Lord Bortimar despises him." He paused, then admitted, "And me."

And there it was. Everything Hamel hated about these people.

He sighed. "My lord, do you know why I make a living traveling from place to place and playing for scraps and trifles, when I could have had a position at any court I wished when I graduated?"

Mineus looked intrigued. He shook his head.

"Because you noble types are constantly squabbling and maneuvering for just a little bit more, and don't pay any attention to the common people who get stepped on when you do. I had someone close to me destroyed by this kind of scheming and I'll have no more of it." He downed the last of his wine and held the empty glass out toward the hireling, because why not. "So I will thank you for the wine and ask you to have your man take me back to my flat. The answer is no."

The hireling didn't move to take Hamel's glass, though his brow did twitch ever so slightly. Hopefully in amusement, or things could get real painful later.

Lord Mineus looked silently at Hamel for a long moment. Then he made the slightest of shrugs and raised his glass to his lips again. He sipped, and looked back into the fire. "I happen to know there is another Isenholf in Mangin City at the moment.'

Hamel froze again, and his guts went to ice.

"Corporal Theobald Isenholf. Formerly of the Crown's Army. Until he deserted and incited an entire platoon to do the same. He then took to thieving and banditry. Murder. He held the entire town of Lydelton hostage, and killed their Constable." Mineus shook his head. "The depositions the new Constables of Glimmer Vale gave are full of vivid details. And theirs are not the only ones." His eyes went back to meeting Hamel's. They were hard as diamonds. "Were he my brother, I would want to put as much distance between myself and him as I could. I certainly wouldn't come to the city where he was imprisoned and plot to break him out of jail before he can be tried."

By the Gods, he knew. He knew everything.

Mineus' eyes narrowed. "What if I told you I could get the crown to hear his appeal? And that on the way to the Capital the Marshalls escorting him could be made to meet with…an accident."

"If Lord Bortimar consents to let your son marry his daughter."

Mineus nodded. "Yes."

Hamel swallowed, despite the fact that his mouth had just gone completely dry.

His mind raced. What Mineus had just suggested…it was not treason, but it came close. Springing a criminal from the Crown's custody, and killing the Crown's Marshalls in the process…

Hell, it bloody well *was* treason.

Hamel looked quickly to the side, toward the hireling. He hadn't changed his posture at all, but there was something different about him, a feeling of pent-up tension, like a bow pulled back and ready to loose.

Hamel could refuse. But then the arrow would fly.

He could accept. And then the arrow would fly after the job was done. Either way, he was screwed.

But…Theo. If there was any chance this could help his big brother…

"You arrange the appeal tomorrow, before I do anything."

Mineus studied him briefly, then shrugged. "Certainly."

Hamel brought the wine glass back in front of himself and looked down at its emptiness for a second. Then he looked back at Mineus.

"In that case, I'd say I need some more of that wine."

Lord Mineus smiled, and it was a smile of victory.

They didn't let him leave the town house.

Hamel wasn't surprised by that, and if circumstances had been different he wouldn't have minded it at all. Even the servants' quarters would have been more comfortable than the dismal flat he rented across the street from the jailhouse. But the notion that Lord Mineus could decide to limit his personal risk and have the silent but deadly hireling kill him, and to blazes with this silly idea to marry his son to Lord Bortimar's daughter, made the stay less than comfortable.

Of course, they didn't put him in the servants' quarters. The Lord gave him a guest room, more opulent than anything Hamel had seen since he left the Academy, with a bed as thick and soft as a cloud and blankets that felt like bliss itself.

He just wished he could have actually enjoyed it.

Hamel racked his brain for as long as he could that night before sleep pummeled him into submission, and then the entire next day.

How to get a man who hated Lord Mineus and his son to feel even a little affection for them?

Hamel had no idea. But considering it had to require more than just a little affection for Lord Bortimar to give his maiden daughter to Lord Mineus' son, his no idea wasn't even adequate as a start.

But then, it didn't have to be love. It just had to be politically or economically advantageous.

Hamel shoved that thought away. There was no more political or economic advantage for Lord Bortimar to gain here. Unless he cast his aging and now most likely barren wife aside and took a new maiden as his wife in the hope of producing another heir— and who knew if the Lord was even capable of such a thing anymore at his age—his estate would transfer to someone not of his blood.

Unless he married his daughter well. Or not even well, just at all.

When looked at pragmatically, there wasn't a much better

choice for her than young Stepan. His house was strong and wealthy. And when he inherited, the combined might of both lines would forge an even stronger dynasty that could come to dominate the politics of the entire northern part of the Kingdom.

But there was that pesky problem of Lord Bortimar despising both of the Mineus men.

The simple math of the situation had to be going through Lord Bortimar's mind. Hamel just had to figure a way to push the antagonism aside, even for just a short while, so the logic could win out. Even just for a moment. Because once Lord Bortimar acknowledged the benefits of the pairing, especially since Lucilla had good feelings for Stepan already, he would find it very hard to go back to being adamantly opposed to the idea.

And then, over time, with the normal coaxing of interpersonal relations and not magic…who knows?

The problem was how to do that. By sunset of the next night, the night before the ball, Hamel still had no clue how to make it happen.

When sleep finally took him, Hamel was awash with frustration and dread. He was certain that Lord Mineus would not just simply let him walk away if he failed.

Hell, even if he succeeded.

But with success came perhaps a chance to get out with his skin. Failure meant only death, for both him and his brother.

His dreams were brief and brought him no rest. When the servants shook him awake and bad him hurry to get ready for the move back to the manor house, he felt as though he hadn't laid down at all.

Lord Mineus held the ball at his manor house in the forest west of the city. The town house simply didn't have sufficient room to support the kind of event he wanted to throw, and at first glance Hamel couldn't blame him. The Ball was to honor the Royal

Marshalls, after all. After the Army, there was no more honorable and revered organization in the Kingdom. They upheld justice and the law, and...

And they were going to escort Hamel's brother to his death, unless he met Lord Mineus' demands.

That made it hard for Hamel to feel quite so good about the Marshalls.

The Mineus' manor house had a grand ballroom, with high, arched ceilings that some painter of considerable skill had spent what had to have been a long and very uncomfortable time painting frescos of birds of all kinds soaring through white puffy clouds in a bright blue sky. A long wall of windows looked outside to a grassy hill that swept down from the manor house to the small lake where the Lord kept a trio of pleasure boats tied up to a long white-painted dock that thrust out into the lake like a spear. The room was lit by a trio of hanging candelabras the size of two men lying heel to head, and there was room for a full orchestra on a stage on the far end of the room from the entrance side, so the attendees could dance on finely cut and almost seamlessly mated marble stones to any tune imaginable.

Hamel didn't get stationed there.

Instead, Lord Mineus put him in a side room. Still spacious and floored in marble, though with lower ceilings and lacking the frescos of the main room, and windowless, it nevertheless had more than enough room for a couple dozen people to mingle and dance. But Mineus stationed some of his broad-shouldered hirelings on either side of the archway leading into this room from the main ballroom, and the wine and food set out on a blue-clothed table that took up the entire length of one wall were a few notches above that which was dispersed in the big room.

Everyone Lord Mineus invited to the Ball was important, at least in their own minds. This room was for the truly important people.

Hamel picked at the doublet the head servant had given him earlier in the afternoon and shook his head in discontent. The doublet was plain blue, like all the servants' and like the cloth on his room's table, and had the coat of arms of House Mineus on the breast. Just like the fellow who had opened the door to the town house.

Hamel hated it. He was no servant.

But he did have to admit it made for a good disguise. Had he come in his own performance best attire, he would have stood out and everyone would remember him. In this outfit, if he was lucky and did his job right no one would remember him at all except as the nameless harpist and singer in the corner. A highly skilled harpist and singer, or he wouldn't have been in with the real people.

But still, no one to truly be noted.

That was good. Even though the outfit itself was horrible.

The guests began arriving before sunset, and mostly kept to mingling in the grand ballroom and eating the finger foods and morsels that servants brought around for the first hour or so as they watched the sun lower over the lake and then fall beneath the tree line. Then, as if on cue, the orchestra took up playing and the ballroom floor cleared, the first of the couples stepping out to dance.

That opened the floodgates into Hamel's room. Before long, there were half a dozen couples stepping to the beat of his music in the center of the room, and at least a dozen more mingling and gossiping in the periphery.

One and all were dressed in outfits that probably cost more than the average man earned in a year. Disgusting as that was, Hamel had to admit it made them look good. Especially the women.

Memories flooded back to him as he played and they played back, of his time at the Academy and immediately thereafter. Of attending Balls like this in the Capital, learning etiquette and dance, practicing seduction along with his music. And for a time he missed that world.

Until he remembered the friend he'd lost to it.

That memory almost made him stand up and leave, but then he caught sight of Lord Mineus, clad in a black-and silver doublet and cape with his house's coat of arms on the breast, a thick black leather belt cinched about his waist, loose grey leggings again, and polished calf-high black boots.

He was walking with a young man who could only have been his son.

Stepan had the same cheekbones and black hair, though without the grey of course, and although he stood half a hand taller than his father he carried himself in the same way. His attire was different though: forest green to his father's black, with brown belt and boots to go with it.

Hamel had to admit he was a good-looking fellow.

He cast about, looking for the other half of his mark. But there were so many ladies he had no idea who could have been -

"Ah, Lucilla," Lord Mineus said loudly, more loudly than perhaps he needed to, and it drew Hamel's attention his way. "Lovely to see you again."

Hamel picked her out immediately. She was petite, but Mineus was correct; she was striking. Flowing blonde locks that were held back from her face by a silver tiara. A cream and silver dress that was snug in all the right places to accentuate her curves, and a wide, generous smile that didn't quite reach her eyes.

The eyes were the only mar on her beauty. They were puffy, as though she had been crying recently.

Of course she had; her brother had just been killed.

She curtsied to Lord Mineus, and he kissed the back of her hand. When she did the same to Stepan, he hesitated to make the kiss, and she hesitated to rise. They just looked at each other for a little bit.

Mineus had understated the situation. They did not just have kind feelings for each other; they were smitten.

Hamel had the idea this wouldn't be nearly as difficult as he had feared when a scowling, rail-thin old man with a thinning silver hair and a hooked nose and wearing a deep red coat and black leggings, stepped up beside Lucilla and, wielding the silver-headed cane he used to move around with, made to knock Stepan about the head.

The young Lordling yelped and moved away from Lord Bortimar—for who else could it have been—and this daughter, and the cane lowered.

Mineus frowned and stepped forward, saying something in a lower tone that Hamel couldn't hear.

Bortimar replied, and he shook his cane forcefully to accentuate his words. Then he took his daughter's arm and led her away.

As she left, she looked over her shoulder at Stepan, and Hamel could see the apology on her face.

So much for easy.

Hamel was watching the father and daughter weave through the crowd when he heard a throat clearing at his side. He turned and saw Lord Mineus there.

"You see the problem now, Bard?"

Hamel nodded. He had indeed.

Mineus gave him a meaningful look, then went back to the business of entertaining his guests.

It didn't take very long to remember why Hamel enjoyed playing in Inns and Taverns more than in fancy parties like this one: in the Inns, people actually listen to what you're playing.

Here, unless people were actually trying to dance, they couldn't have cared less. His music and his voice were background noise, to set the ambience, and he was a fixture of decoration, nothing more. There was none of the vibrant interaction with the audience that he had become accustomed to.

Then again, the tips were bigger. So that was nice.

Over the next hour or so, Hamel saw Stepan and Lucilla

several times, but never together. And she was never very far from her father.

Or really the other way around. Old Lord Bortimar seemed obsessed with staying near to his daughter. And whether it was from a normal father doting on his daughter or a reaction to the crushing grief of his recent loss, it was obvious she felt the constant proximity trying.

It was an interesting dynamic, and Hamel began to despair of ever being able to find an opening. So after a while, he stopped trying and just went back to playing and singing.

As always when he opened himself to the song, the energy from the music curled and flowed around and into him, and he grew more energized. His fingers flew across the strings and he sang far past his upper register into falsetto, and the energy built and flowed.

He inflected the lyrics in a spirit-boosting tone, and the conversation around him shifted from quiet and somber to upbeat and boisterous as he fed them energy from the music.

But still the couple did not interact.

Several people requested something brisk that they could really dance too. After a minute's consideration Hamel began playing Charge Of The Blades. Couldn't get more brisk than the ballad of the Battle of Talmor Flats.

The opening verse started slow, but the tempo increased quickly as the battle lines formed and the first volleys were exchanged, archer versus archer across the field.

Hamel could almost see it as he played, and he fed the courage of the combatants our into the audience, willing them to dance without reserve.

And they began to. Couples who before had been stately and reserved now moved with enthusiastic energy. Laughter and whoops even escaped an occasional noble mouth, and Hamel knew he had it going well tonight.

Across the room, he saw Lucilla, and her father was nowhere in sight.

Quickly finding Stepan elsewhere in the crowd and seeing that he was looking her way, Hamel raised his voice in a quick crescendo and focused the energy of courage toward the young man.

He moved forward. Lucilla saw him coming and smiled. This time the smile reached her eyes.

And then she was swept away. A fellow Hamel didn't know grabbed her by the arm and whisked her out onto the floor, with the other dancing couples.

No real harm; dance partners shifted throughout the night. But it wouldn't do to have Stepan get disheartened, so after Charge Of The Blades, Hamel moved into Umalt's Last Stand, a ballad about Umalt's fight and victory against overwhelming odds.

Quick movement from the dance floor took Hamel's gaze away from Stepan, and he saw Lucilla and her dance partner...not dancing. She was trying to pull away, but he was grabbing at her arms, not willing to let her go.

She gave a jerk and managed to wrench free, but she overbalanced and fell over onto her backside, her dress and petticoats coming all out of sorts.

A gasp went out from the others in the room, and all eyes turned toward the former couple, trying to see what had happened.

Hamel stopped playing himself, so surprised was he at this turn of events.

And so he heard the fellow's mocking laughter at Lucilla's upset situation quite clearly. Her cheeks flushed crimson from embarrassment as she tried to right herself.

"What do you think you are doing?" The demand came from Stepan, who came up to Lucilla's erstwhile dance partner, accusation in his eyes and anger in his tone.

The fellow looked at Stepan and snorted. "None of your concern, Mineus."

Stepan gave him a baleful glare, then moved to step around

him to where Lucilla still sat. He was holding his hand out to help her up when the other fellow shoved him.

Stepan stumbled forward, but righted himself and turned around. Just in time for the man to throw a jab at his jaw.

As the young nobleman took the hit, Hamel could only watch in stunned amazement. He had never seen a squabble like this, one that came to fisticuffs, in noble company before. A duel the next morning? Sure.

But fisticuffs on the dance floor? This was unheard of.

He had played several martial and aggressive ballads in a row, and had been pushing the energy out as intensely as he could, trying to get the couple's courage levels up. But he hadn't really thought about the affect that would have on everyone else present. And this new fellow clearly was a hothead to start with... now he was worse.

Another jab, but this time Stepan caught it. He had his hands up in a guard now, and though his bottom lip was bleeding he was in control of himself.

"Calm down, Tomas," he said, clearly as baffled by what was going on as anyone else.

Tomas just snarled and launched a right hook punch at Stepan's head.

Stepan ducked beneath it then countered with a hook of his own into Tomas' side. Then an uppercut to his belly.

Tomas doubled over, and a hook to his temple put him on the floor.

The room was silent for several seconds, then the onlookers began clapping in appreciation for Stepan's performance. Even Lucilla on the floor looked as though her earlier embarrassment had faded beneath admiration for the feat.

"Well," a gruff, elderly voice said from off to the right. Hamel looked over and saw Lord Bortimar at the edge of the crowd. He was leaning on his cane next to Lord Mineus, and from the look of things had watched the entire confrontation. He looked sidelong at Mineus and continued, "Boy's got more gumption than I gave him credit for. You sure he's yours?"

Mineus' jaw dropped open, in shocked surprise turning to disbelief then to anger over the insult.

But Lord Bortimar didn't notice. He caned his way over to where Stepan was now helping Lucilla to her feet. He nudged the young man aside with his cane, and Stepan complied, the pride of victory that had just been filing him giving way to resignation as the old Lord again did what he always did.

Lord Bortimar asked, "Are you all right, my dear?" and Lucilla nodded.

Her enthusiasm had faded as well, and she looked at her father with trepidation.

The old Lord nodded as though to say, "Good." Then he turned to look at Stepan more directly. "Good work, boy. Might be a man within you after all."

He offered his daughter his arm, and he led her out of the room.

Two of the broad-shouldered hirelings entered then, quite a bit too late. They looked at Tomas, who had recovered some of his senses but was still on the floor, groaning, then at Lord Mineus.

He grunted and gestured at the troublemaker. "Throw him out."

As the hirelings moved to do that, Mineus met Hamel's eyes, and he nodded.

The guests began to leave around midnight, first sneaking away in ones or twos and then in larger groups until finally, about two bells into the new day there remained only the last half-dozen or so people who were either too stupid or too inebriated to realize the party was over.

Lord Mineus' broad-shouldered hirelings saw them out with remarkable gentleness, and then there was only Hamel, the servants who were beginning the work of cleaning up, and the hirelings.

Hamel had to admit, he felt kind of good, despite his fatigue. The remainder of the evening had gone very differently for the hoped-for couple. Stepan and Lucilla danced together twice. Lord Bortimar watched closely, but without nearly the disapproval he had at the beginning of the night. And certainly without the inclination to draw her away as quickly as he could once the dance was over.

It seemed whatever had caused the altercation—and Hamel still was not sure whether he actually had anything to do with it or not—it had broken the ice a bit. When Lord Bortimar and Lucilla departed, it wasn't without Stepan asking for and getting permission to call on her later in the week.

The young lordling went off to bed with a broad smile on his face that hadn't been there before, and that had been reflected in Lord Mineus' as he watched his son depart.

The old Lord could dress the hoped-for marriage up as a political play all he wanted, but Hamel was convinced he really saw that his son was in love and wanted to do whatever he could to help Stepan find happiness. And if that meant ingratiating them with their biggest rival…so be it.

It was rather touching, in its own way.

"Bard." The gravelly voice of Rubert, the silent but deadly hireling came from over his shoulder, and Hamel turned from where he had been cleaning his harp. "My lord will see you at the dock," Rubert said, gesturing toward one of the doors leading out to the grounds.

Hamel nodded and took a moment to put the harp in its case and sling it over his shoulder, then proceeded outside.

As he descended the hill toward the dock, he could make out Lord Mineus standing alone on the shore and not on the white wooden planks that made up the dock itself. The entire place was gloomy, the moon having set not long before so the only illumination was from the stars and light shining down from the manor house itself.

The dark made Hamel's mood shift from self-congratulatory happiness to wariness. It could be that the Lord just wanted to ensure no one observed their interaction, so no word could make it to any of his rivals.

Or it could be the bow was about to be loosed in Hamel's back.

Hamel glanced behind and was unsurprised to see Rubert trailing a few steps back.

That was hardly comforting.

He stopped in front of Lord Mineus and looked at the older man. He was looking out at the still waters of the lake as if lost in thoughts.

Hamel cleared his throat and the Lord gave a little start. He met Hamel's gaze and made a little smile and a shrug as though to say, "You got me," before speaking.

"I think that went rather well."

Hamel nodded. "Yes, my lord. I won't venture to say your troubles are completely past with Lord Bortimar. But it's a start."

Mineus nodded. "I agree." He reached beneath his cape and pulled out a pouch. Holding it out to Hamel, he said, "For your troubles."

Hamel accepted the pouch and bounced it in his hand once. It was reassuringly heavy, and it clinked.

Excellent. But that wasn't why he'd done this.

"My brother?"

"His appeal was sent to the crown by pigeon this morning. My associate in the Capital will approve it, and the Marshalls should receive word within the week."

Hamel nodded. As Lord Mineus had promised. Of course, he only had the nobleman's word, but Hamel had a lot of practice reading people, and fishing out truth from lies.

This one felt like the truth.

"And where will he be released?"

Lord Mineus said nothing, and Hamel realized the idiocy of

his question. Even if Mineus knew where the event would take place, he couldn't admit to it. Just in case.

But something told Hamel he would get the word, one way or another.

"Well, I guess that makes us square." Hamel made a full bow this time. However he might feel about the situation, it seemed appropriate to at least go with the proper formalities here, at the end. "My lord."

Lord Mineus inclined his head in response to the bow. "Good luck, Master Isenholf." Then he turned and walked up the hill, passing his hireling as he went.

Rubert did not move, not for several seconds until the Lord was well away and out of clear view.

Then he stepped forward, toward Hamel.

So that's how it was, after all.

He drew a breath. "I guess this is the part where you kill me." Rubert remained silent, but took another step toward him. "To protect your Lord's secrets."

Hamel backed away, and his foot came down on the wooden planks of the dock. Rubert kept coming.

"I won't say a thing, you know," he said. "What would I get out of it?"

More backpedalling, and he made it up the shallow ramp to the flat portion that ran out to where the boats were tied.

Rubert said in his gravelly voice, "If it makes you feel any better, he keeps his promises." His foot came down on the wood of the dock. "You brother will go free."

"Great. So he only double-crosses one Isenholf tonight."

The corners of Rubert's mouth turned ever so slightly upward. "He never promised you would."

Hamel had to admit, Rubert had a fair point. He looked over his shoulder and saw that he was almost out of dock space, and Rubert was almost upon him.

For a second, he thought maybe to try to fight against the hireling. But as he looked back at Rubert he new immediately it would be a lost cause. The way he moved, every aspect of his persona, spoke of training and intent that surpassed Hamel's in every conceivable way.

Hamel sighed. At least Theo would be alright. "Just make it quick."

In a flash, Rubert was on him. Even if he had tried to resist, there would have been nothing Hamel could have done to stop him.

Hamel's arms were pinned and locked behind his back and he felt himself being lifted off his feet.

Rubert's breath came hot and steady on the side of his neck. He spoke again. "Set foot in Mangin City again, and you will never see the next dawn."

Then Hamel was flying head over heels.

The water of the lake embraced him like a lover, and he sank down to the bottom.

***

Hamel looked over his shoulder at the retreating walls of Mangin City, and wished the wagon he was riding could go faster.

After he had sputtered his way out of the lake, he had not bothered to try to get a ride from anyone in Lord Mineus' household. He simply ran, clutching the pouch of coins that he had somehow held onto throughout his foray into the water, and his harp case.

He ran until his legs shook and he thought he would fall over and sleep for a week.

Then he ran some more.

He finally reached the gates of the city as dawn was breaking over the Saddleback Mountains to the west, and he actually had to wait almost a half hour before the Watch's morning shift came on duty and they opened the gates for the day.

Then he ran to his flat and gathered his things.

An hour later he was in the warehouse section of the city, and found a traveling merchant who was departing for places south. A quick exchange of coin and Hamel was aboard, and not a moment too soon.

Now that he was out of the city, fatigue fully hit him and he slumped in his seat, his eyelids heavy.

He was just beginning to drift off when his hand came down on the satchel that contained all of his worldly goods except his harp case and he felt an unfamiliar hard shape. His mind made the connection to the pouch the Lord had given him, and he jerked back awake.

He had never actually looked inside it; he had paid the merchant with money from his own pouch, earned the other night at the Juggling Gypsy.

Hamel fished the Lord's pouch out of the satchel and untied the laces holding it shut.

He opened it, and gold glinted in the sunlight. Hamel gasped and immediately closed it up. Gold was not something you wanted to be showing people, or at least people you didn't know.

But looking over at the merchant, who was intent on driving his mules, it seemed he could take one more look.

Yes, it was gold. Gold, and a scrap of parchment.

Hamel fished the parchment out. There was writing on it, in a neat and meticulous hand.

"Heartspring Inn. Oberton."

Hamel didn't know the Inn, but he had heard of Oberton. It was a small village about halfway to the Capital.

That was where Theo would be, so that's where Hamel was going.

He turned to look ahead, and realized the arrow had been loosed, all right. He had loosed it himself.

WEDDING GIFTS

A GLIMMER VALE CHRONICLES STORY

MICHAEL KINGSWOOD

AUTHOR OF *THE PERICLES CONSPIRACY*

WEDDING GIFTS

It's three hours until the wedding of Raedrick Baletier to Lani Millens, and Melanie Klemins doesn't have a present for them.

Or rather, she did. But she lost it.

Now it's up to Julian Hinderbrook to find the gift and retrieve it, or the wedding will be ruined and the couple's magical day tarnished forever.

Wedding Gifts takes place between Robbed Blind (Glimmer Vale Chronicles #4) and The Falconer's Stairs (Glimmer Vale Chronicles #5).

"Julian, I need your help."

Julian Hinderbrook put down his tankard and turned in his chair to look at the speaker.

He knew it was Melanie before he saw her. No other woman had her relatively deep voice and refined manner of speech, not in Lydelton at least. And no one else had that way of making a request seem a command. Though, truth to tell, he and his fellow Constable, Raedrick Baletier, had come to her requesting help far more often than she had come to them.

It was full Spring now in Glimmer Vale, and the townsfolk of Lydelton had removed their winter layers eagerly. Melanie was no exception this day, wearing a simple but elegant deep blue gown that was laced at the cuffs, hem, and neckline with silver-white thread. A similarly stitched belt cinched the gown in at her waist, accentuating as always the curve of her hips even as it supported the knife she always seemed to wear.

She was a sight to see, between that lush figure, the wavy dark brown hair that hung to just past her shoulders, and the blue eyes that flashed with intelligence and could just draw a man in if he was not careful. Ordinarily, Julian would be forced to take a moment to admire her beauty, but the worried expression on her face gave him pause.

"What do you need?" He gestured at the empty chair at his table.

Melanie sat, but paused to glance over her shoulder toward where Molli Millens stood over by the bar that ran most of the length of the other side of the taproom from Julian's table. The Oarlock's proprietor, and mother of the bride-to-be, was dressed in her usual flowery dress covered by a white apron, and she beamed with happiness as she chivvied her similarly-aproned barmaids around in their efforts to ready the taproom of The Oarlock for the night's festivities.

Molli had gone all out for it. Flowers of all sorts were strung up on lines that spanned the width of the taproom, and the bar had been scrubbed until the darkly-stained wood of its countertop gleamed in the sunlight that spilled in through the open windows at the front of the room. The two fireplaces, opposite each other near the front, were clear of ashes and soot stains, filled instead with more flowers in pots. The small stage that she set up most evenings for performances was draped in a white cloth, with a polished steel trellis center-stage where the high priest would give his blessings.

And of course it wouldn't be Molli Millens' place without a mouth-watering blend of scents pouring out from the kitchens at the rear. Spiced fish, fried potatoes, and stewed beef overlaid a veritable cornucopia of goodness that made Julian wish he hadn't just finished lunch.

"Have you gotten a gift for Raedrick and Lani yet?"

Melanie's question drew Julian's attention back to her, and he blinked. That was not the sort of question he expected. "Uh... Yes, why? Haven't you?"

Melanie flushed slightly.

He could only stare in disbelief. "Melanie, the wedding's in three hours!"

The flush increased, but the level look Melanie directed at him was more irritated than embarrassed. "I am well aware of that. It's -"

One of the few barmaids that Molli let get about her normal duties today arrived right then, and Melanie clamped her mouth shut in a little scowl.

"Get you something, Mistress Klemins?" the girl, a homely blonde just off her mother's purse strings named Telli, said, and actually bobbed a little curtsy.

For a second Julian thought Melanie was going to give Telli the rough side of her tongue, but she visibly pulled her irritation back and shook her head. "No, thank you."

Telli nodded and made another curtsy, then flashed Julian a quick smile before hurrying off to the only other occupied table in the front section of the taproom, where four grey-cloaked fishing men from the night shift were having their dinner in front of one of the fireplaces.

A cleared throat from Melanie prompted Julian to turn away from watching Telli depart. "You were saying?"

"Yes." Melanie drew in a breath. "Lani made Raedrick a new winter cloak, did you know that? With her own two hands."

Julian shook his head. "Wow."

"Indeed. She showed it to me shortly after it was made, and I had an idea. She gave me permission to try, and..." She stopped and fixed him with another one of her trademark level looks. "Do you remember what I told you about magical constructs?"

"Pretty much. You put the components of the spell inside the thing and it can do the spell."

She smirked. "There is a bit more to it than that, but close enough. Anyway, I've been researching these constructs since we tussled with Job and Iben."

Julian couldn't help but scowl at the mention of the two corrupt Royal Marshalls. They had robbed the Covington Brothers' Fishing Company and nearly brought Lydelton's economy to its knees, and only quick action and a bit of magical assistance from Melanie had allowed him and Raedrick to catch them before they could make their escape.

Melanie continued, "I believe I've worked out the trick to it. I resolved to enchant the brooch for Raedrick's new cloak so that it would create heat within the cloak itself."

"You're kidding."

Melanie shook her head. "It seemed so easy, so simple. What could go wrong?"

Oh no. Julian saw where this was going. "You burned up the cloak, didn't you?"

"What? No, of course not!" Melanie looked offended for a second, but then that faded and became full-on embarrassment. She looked away, avoiding Julian's eyes. "No. The cloak...flew away out my window."

Julian just sat there, gaping at her, speechless.

Several seconds passed, then Melanie looked back at him and her irritated scowl returned. "Close your mouth before you swallow a fly."

Instead of doing that, Julian took a long drag on his tankard. He swallowed a mouthful of Molli's signature ale and slowly lowered the tankard back onto his table again, then finally spoke. "The cloak flew away."

Melanie nodded.

"Of its own accord."

Another nod.

He couldn't help it, he burst out in laughter. Oh, that was too rich!

"Julian."

He slapped the table, still laughing, and had to pinch his eyes shut to hold back tears of mirth.

"Julian, this is serious."

He tried to respond, but looking at her steadily deeper flushing cheeks sent another spasm of laughter through him.

"Julian!" She slapped the table herself. Hard, and not out of mirth.

That combined with the ice in her eyes stopped his laughter. Mostly.

He held up a finger, requesting a moment, then took another quick drink. "Well, you *have* got a problem there. What do you need me to do?"

"Find it, of course!"

He blinked innocently at her. "Melanie, I'm the Constable, not a finder of flying cloaks."

"Do you think I would ask you if it wasn't important?" Her voice all of a sudden was a mixture of consternation and near desperation.

Julian looked at her more closely, and realized that she was well and truly upset. Those level looks, the icy stare...those had just been a mask. That tightness around her eyes was genuine fear that she had just ruined Lani's wedding day.

He reached out and laid his hand on her shoulder. Giving it a gentle squeeze, he said. "Don't worry, we'll find it."

Melanie gave a quick shake of her head. "We? No, I said I need *you* to find it."

"Hold on a second here. I'm willing to help, but - "

"I figured out the mistake I made in the enchantment, but I need time to prepare the correction. Bring the cloak back to my shop in the next hour and a half, and I should be able to fix it in time for the ceremony."

He snorted. "Don't you think it would be best to just leave enchantments alone at this point? Give them a pot or something?"

She looked at him like he was daft.

Finally, after a long several seconds that felt like several minutes, Julian rolled his eyes toward the ceiling and threw his hands up. "Fine. I'll find the doubly-cursed cloak." Draining the last of his tankard, he stood, grabbed up his baldric and scabbard from where it had been leaning against his table, and slipped the baldric over his shoulder. "Don't suppose you know where it is?"

Melanie shook her head. "It flew off to the northwest."

"Great. Well, I'd best get to it then."

Melanie smiled at him.

He turned away from the table and took a step toward The Oarlock's front door.

"Remember. An hour and a half. No longer."

Julian looked back over his shoulder and smirked. "Don't you trust me, Melanie?"

She just gave him a level look in return.

Against his better judgment, he found he was laughing again as he walked out the door.

Julian received no fewer than a dozen quizzical looks from townsfolk as he departed The Oarlock and traversed Lydelton's streets to the west and north, asking if anyone had seen a flying cloak.

The odd looks would have been tolerable, but one older fellow, a retired blacksmith if Julian recalled correctly, asked whether he had taken a blow to the head.

Julian stopped asking after that, just trudged up the paving stones of Main Street, muttering to himself and keeping his eyes raised to the sky, searching for any hint of the cloak. He quickly lost the feeling of amusement he had when he departed The Oarloack and was steadily getting more and more irritated.

It was completely understandable that Melanie would want to experiment with her new discoveries. But now? With this?

Normally she was pretty level-headed. What was she thinking?

He only realized he was scowling when a young lad, running full out from a side street, turned toward him and, seeing his face, turned and ran the other way.

Julian sighed and shook his head at his own silliness. No sense getting in a huff over this. After all, it truly was more amusing than anything else, if he thought about it honestly.

He picked up the pace, continuing down Main Street and looking to and fro.

If I were a flying cloak, where would I hide?

That was the question, and Julian pondered it for two blocks before he came up with a possible answer.

The same place birds do: corners of rooftops, steeples, lamps, things like that.

Stopping, he turned a full circle, carefully examining the buildings in that area of town. Most were low, single or two stories, with sharply pointing roofs designed to allow the heavy snowfall that came during the Vale's winters to slide off easily.

That left some nice nooks and crannies to hide in. But where...?

Ah ha!

Bigsbe's Boarding House, back a street or two from Main Street, though two stories tall itself, was still a fair bit taller than its surrounding neighbors. It had a long roof, and was just about on a direct northwest line from Melanie's Mystical Crafts.

Feeling more cheerful now that he had a target to aim at, Julian turned off of Main Street and its paving stones, and onto the packed earth of Lydelton's side streets. A quick right and then a left, and he stood before the Boarding House's front entrance.

Ok, now what?

He slowly paced the length of the building, squinting upwards at the eaves. It made sense that the cloak might...

There.

Over at the leftmost corner of the building, where the roof abruptly changed direction, something dark was hanging in the eaves. Hanging...like a bat. Except bats weren't out in the open in the middle of the day.

The thing fluttered slightly as the breeze took it, and Julian grinned in triumph.

Got it.

That left just how to get it down. He peered about, but the side street was clear of boxes, carts, or other things he could stand on. The Boarding House's stairs were inside the building, and the corner was far enough from the closest windows that it wouldn't do him any good to try that route.

So, no getting up to it. Maybe he could knock it down. There were any number of small stones lying about on the side of the street.

Worth a shot.

Julian grabbed up a couple, took aim, and let fly.

The first rock missed wide, but his second struck true, right up by the eaves where the cloak presumably was caught.

It fell, drifting slowly down to the ground like a leaf falling from a tree. Julian grinned and moved quickly to get below it.

And received the shock of his life.

Halfway down, the cloak stretched out taut. Then it rolled over on itself and dove straight at him.

Flummoxed, Julian could only watch in complete shock as the thing engulfed him in its black length. It wrapped him up tight, and for a second it almost felt as though the thing was going to pick him up off the ground. Then it let him go and he fell.

More like it threw him to the ground.

He landed on his backside and bit his tongue hard. He bellowed out a curse and clutched at his hurt mouth while pushing himself up onto his feet again.

Just in time to see the cloak winging its way upwards until it was level with the rooftops. It leveled and paused in midair for a moment, then zoomed off to the west.

"Son of a bitch," Julian breathed.

Then he set off running after it.

The cloak led him a merry chase, out past the outskirts of town and beyond toward the thick pines of the Glamorwood, and the jagged mountains beyond. Several times, Julian was able to get close enough to wing it with another rock, but each time the cloak was only slowed for an extremely short period of time, not enough for him to catch up fully.

It flew ahead of him over the tall grass that grew between Lydelton and the woods, and Julian began to think that he would not ever catch the cursed thing before it reached the forest. And once it reached the woods, the gig would be up.

To hell with that. This was his best friend and partner's wedding present from his bride!

Julian picked up the pace, fairly sprinting up a shallow rise as the cloak seemed to slow briefly.

He approached the summit. The cloak was much closer now. Maybe he could...

He leapt for all he was worth, stretching his arms upwards and forwards. His fingertips brushed the trailing edge of the garment for a heartbeat.

And then it was gone, and he fell flat onto his face on the downslope of the hill. He rolled twice before coming to a halt, then just lay there for a moment, hurting in about a dozen different places.

Overhead, it seemed the cloak actually was mocking him, as it did a slow circle for a few seconds before flying away again, this time more fully west than its previous northwesterly route.

A big chunk of Julian just wanted to stay there, on his back in the grass, and recover for a while.

Not a chance.

He forced himself up onto his feet, then trotted up to the next rise, trying to ignore a twinge in his left knee. At the top, he looked to the west, and blinked in surprise.

A long, low, thatch-roofed building stood there near the edge of the forest: Lydelton's old Ranger Station. Julian hadn't gone near the place in months, and he had almost forgotten it was there. Sure, part of the town's budget went to maintaining it, even though no Rangers were currently stationed there. But that wasn't his and Raedrick's department, and so he had just...not thought about it.

A fluttering black shape veered toward the Ranger Station. The cloak.

Thank the Gods it wasn't heading straight into the woods. If it stopped at the Station...

And sure enough, as it got closer to the building, the cloak dove for its roof.

Curious, that. But Julian wasn't about to let the oddness of the flying cloak's behavior get in the way of his gratitude that it appeared to have stopped moving again.

He hurried down toward the Ranger Station as quickly as he could without making his knee hurt even worse.

When he reached the Ranger Station, he peered closely at its roof and grinned. The black cloak would surely stand out against the yellow-brown of the thatch. It oughtn't take long to find the thing.

And yet, after a complete circuit of the building, he couldn't see it anywhere.

Muttering under his breath, he considered that the cloak may have just ducked down near the Ranger Station, but continued on into the Glamorwood beyond. He glanced up at the sun, beginning its oh-so-brief descent from its zenith to the eastern horizon. He only had a few minutes more to find the cloak or he would miss Melanie's deadline and the gift would be ruined, regardless.

All the same, he had no intention of going into those woods after the damn thing. Not by himself.

So he started to circle back around the building, looking closely up at the rooftop again. And then he saw it.

Up under the overhang, near the peak of the roof, there was a gap between the thatch and the stones that made up the building's wall.

Had the cloak forced itself through that hole?

It seemed inconceivable. But there was no other sign of the garment, and Julian could not very well go back without at least checking to be sure.

There was no way he could fit through that hole, small as it was, and no way to get himself up that high regardless, so Julian proceeded around to the Ranger Station's front door.

He fully expected the door to be locked, and he was not disappointed. Fortunately, the door had an older latch-style knob, and the locks on those were relatively easy to get around.

Julian reached into his belt pouch for the tools he would need, but paused as the inanity of his situation came to the forefront of his mind. He was about to pick the lock on a government building to retrieve a cloak that had been flying on its own through half of town, and which he had been chasing like a lunatic the whole way.

If it hadn't actually happened to him, he never would have believed it.

Shaking his head, Julian chuckled softly and set to work on the lock.

A couple minutes later, the door swung inward on squeaky hinges, and Julian stepped inside.

Within, the Ranger Station was all shadows and dust. Light streamed in through the open door, and more dimly through a pair of windows in the back that were partially covered by curtains. The main room, which took up most of the building's interior, was empty for the most part. Desks, a couple tables, and a collection of chairs sat in a neat stack off to his right. To the left, in the direction of the hole the cloak (hopefully) came in, a single door lead into a squared-off partition that did not reach all the way to the roof. Julian presumed that would have been the Chief Ranger's office.

A thick layer of dust covered everything, and rose in small puffs with each step he took. The place smelled musty, as though it had not been disturbed in years.

And it probably hadn't. The town may have been keeping the place up, but only the outside, from the look of things.

He moved further into the building and peered about, squinting as he looked for his quarry.

It had to be in here.

He hoped.

A third of the way through a circuit of the main room, he saw it. In the rafters above the Chief's office, again dangling like a bat.

Julian frowned, considering the layout for a moment.

The Chief's Office was squared-off, and looked to have a separate ceiling. If he could get atop it, he could grab the cloak and that would be that.

Blessing the people who left the tables and chairs there, he crossed the room and, after a few minutes' work, had a table moved over next to the office.

Julian rubbed his hands together and got up onto the table, but after stretching up on his tip-toes, he could only get his fingertips atop the wall.

Not enough to pull himself up the rest of the way.

So he went, got a chair, brought it over, and set it on top of the table.

That did the trick. With more huffing and puffing than he

would have liked, he was able to hoist himself up far enough to get first his elbows and then a foot up onto the office's ceiling.

And then he was up.

He sat there for a moment to get his breath, and resolved to work on his chin-ups more. Back in his Army days, that little climb would not have been so difficult.

Being Constable was too much of a desk job, apparently.

The cloak hung, unmoving, from the corner rafters a couple paces away. If it knew he was there, it showed no sign.

That thought gave him pause, and he took a second to shake his head, again, at his own foolishness. Of course it didn't know he was there! It was a bloody cloak!

He snorted softly, stepped over, and grabbed it.

As soon as his hand closed over it, the cloak came to life. It detached from the rafters and whipped around wildly, jerking to and fro as if trying to make Julian lose his grip.

Which was absurd, of course. Or maybe not. Melanie hadn't been clear exactly what enchantment she had actually laid upon the thing.

Julian grabbed the flapping end of the cloak with his other hand and pulled it down toward his body.

The garment went wild, twisting in his hands and then flinging itself forward to wrap around Julian's head.

"Son of a bitch!"

He stumbled backwards, loosening his grip on the edges of the cloak and grasping at its main body, trying to loose it from his head.

He couldn't see, and breath was rapidly becoming hard to come by. This would not turn out well if he didn't –

His foot came down on nothing, and Julian tumbled backwards.

A split second later, hard wood struck his back, and then the chair gave way beneath his weight. He continued downward, bouncing off the edge of the table until he landed side-first on the floor.

Julian groaned loudly as his entire back and side screamed at him in protest of the fall. He rolled the rest of the way onto his belly and managed to force the cloak away from his face.

There he lay for a long while, panting with exertion and completely ignoring the futile flapping of the cloak, now pinned between his body and the floor.

Melanie had better know how to fix this stupid thing.

She'd better.

Julian pushed the door to Melanie's Mystical Crafts open and limped inside.

The little bell over the door rang, and Melanie, seated behind the counter on the far side of the room to Julian's left, looked up. Seeing him, her eyes went wide.

"What happened to you?"

Julian scowled. Instead of answering, he hobbled past a cabinet full of charms and a few small pamphlets about spirits and ghosts, or something, toward her.

He unceremoniously dumped the cloak, wrapped up and tied into a ball that had been trying to jump out of his hands the entire way back from the Ranger Station, onto the counter.

The cloak bounced up into the air at once, but Melanie quickly caught it. She studied it for a moment before turning her eyes back on Julian.

"Thank you."

"You're welcome. Now if you'll excuse me, I think I'll go start a fist fight with a giant." He turned back toward the door. "It'd hurt less."

Behind him, Melanie half snorted, half chuckled. "See you at the wedding?"

"Yep."

He left.

An hour later, Julian felt a bit better. His knee still hurt and his side throbbed, but at least he could walk without looking like a cripple.

But it was worth it, for this.

He stood behind Raedrick and to his right on the stage that Molli used for musical performances in The Oarlock's taproom.

Raedrick was facing his bride-to-be. She wore the traditional white gown, with her blonde hair tied into two braids that hung down over the front of her shoulders onto her chest, and she was radiant. Her mother stood at her side, and for once Molli wasn't wearing an apron.

Raedrick didn't look too bad either, truth be told. He had on his best: a black doublet lined in silver thread that matched the buckle on his sword belt. His boots were polished enough to be almost mirrors. He had trimmed his goatee. Hell, even the strap he used to tie his black hair into a short ponytail glittered in the lamplight.

The High Priest had not been exactly happy to hold the ceremony here instead of the Temple, but he beamed a joyful smile at the many witnesses that occupied the taproom's many chairs and benches.

As the couple said their oaths, Julian looked out at the crowd, and marveled as he always did at how he and Raedrick had managed to go from two guys on the run to respected leaders in the town, even heroes.

Amazing.

"...the gifts?"

The High Priest's words drew Julian's attention back to the couple.

Raedrick smiled and reached into his belt pouch. A collective gasp issued from the mouths of every lady present when he withdrew the necklace he'd procured for this day. It was simple, and truth be told not super expensive. But it was glittery, and when he fastened it around Lani's neck, it set off her deep blue eyes in exactly the right way.

She smiled broadly, then turned to Molli, who retrieved the bundle that contained Raedrick's cloak.

Julian hadn't noticed, when he was struggling with it earlier, just how nice the cloak was. But now, watching Lani drape it over Raedrick's shoulders and fasten the clasp, Julian was impressed. Fine black wool, lined with grey fur and stitched with grey thread at the hems and around the cowl, with a silver brooch on its left breast in the shape of a clenched fist holding a set of scales. Their badge of office as Constables.

It looked as good or better than some garments Julian had seen noblemen wear.

Raedrick appeared taken aback by the gift, even more so when Lani touched the brooch.

The ornament began to glow for a second, turning a faintly reddish hue that quickly dispersed through the cloak itself before fading completely.

Raedrick's eyebrows rose high on his head, and he turned to look out into the audience in Melanie's direction. But very quickly, his attention returned to his bride, and they shared their first kiss as a family.

Julian joined the rest of the crowd in applause.

In between claps, he glanced out to the crowd and found Melanie. Their eyes met and she smiled with obvious satisfaction.

Julian returned the smile in kind.

LOST CREDIT

A GLIMMER VALE CHRONICLES STORY

MICHAEL KINGSWOOD

AUTHOR OF *THE PERICLES CONSPIRACY*

LOST CREDIT

When one of Lydelton's citizens goes missing after running out on his bar tab, Constable Raedrick Baletier has to track him down.

Lost Credit takes place concurrently with The Falconer's Stairs (Glimmer Vale Chronicles #5).

aedrick Baletier looked up from the parchment he was
reading as the door to the Constabulary swung open,
admitting midday sunlight that brightened the place
more than the lamps hanging on either side of the barred wrought
iron doorway leading back from the front office to the cell block
ever did. His eyes lingered for a second on the empty desk across
the room from his own, adjacent to a small wood stove that would
keep the office at least passingly pleasant in the winter. A rack of
unstrung bows hung on the wall behind the desk, matching a
brace of swords on the wall behind Raedrick's. But the man who
would normally balance out with him was gone.

The new arrival finished stepping inside, and Raedrick
focused in on him.

The man was short and stocky, not quite fat, and had a well-
combed swath of black hair atop his round face. He wore a green
tunic cinched about his waist by a brown leather belt, beige
leggings that were tight to his thighs and calves, and ankle-high
leather boots. Raedrick recognized him as one of the fellows who
worked at Holb's tavern, on the west side of Lydelton past the last
of the docks that put into Lake Glimmermere. But he had never
got the man's name before.

The newcomer also looked at the empty desk for a second
before turning to regard Raedrick fully.

"Morning Constable," he said as the door swung shut, the latch
clicking into place behind him. He made a little gesture with his
left hand toward the empty desk. "Any word from the Deputy?"

Raedrick set the parchment down onto his desk and leaned
back against the carved pine of his chair, the same wood as the
desk was made from, and really the entire building. He shook his
head. "Julian's not my Deputy. We're equal partners."

The man sniffed, and shrugged. "You say so. He on his way
back yet?"

Raedrick had been wondering that very thing for a month
now. Julian had left on a journey with Melanie Klemins and Jared
Tolburt three months ago, on a quest for magical treasure that

shouldn't have taken as long as it already had. And he'd had a difficult time holding down duties as Constable without Julian at his side.

A town of about a thousand adults, in a remote mountain vale weeks away from the closest city, Lydelton was never particularly troublesome. But every now and then a member of a trading caravan would get into a tussle with a local. Or one of the outlying farmsteads would have issues with its neighbor. And then the Mayor wanted his regular reports.

It wasn't a lot of work, most times. But it was never simple or quick to deal with, and it was sometimes tiresome. And with his son—or daughter, but a man can hope—due to arrive any time now, Raedrick was feeling the lack of help.

He returned the man's shrug. "No word, but I expect it won't be much longer." He drew in a breath. "Anyway, what can I do for you, goodman?"

The fellow, though, went back to looking at Julian's empty desk, and frowned.

"Goodman?"

The fellow looked back at Raedrick and smiled apologetically. "Lemmy," he said. "Guess we never did make acquaintance, did we?" He shrugged. "Mostly I come to Julian, seeing as you and Holb don't get along."

Raedrick bristled at that for a moment, but then had to admit Lemmy had a point. He and Holb *had* gotten off on the wrong foot, back when Raedrick and Julian first came to town and took over as Constables of Lydelton, and the rest of Glimmer Vale as well. In fact, Holb had thrown Raedrick out of his tavern—almost literally—during their first meeting. But after that initial misunderstanding they'd been cordial to each other, at least.

All the same he could understand why Holb, and his men, would choose to work with Julian instead of him.

That didn't mean he had to like it.

He managed to hold back a sigh and gave Lemmy a level look. "What seems to be the problem?"

Another quick glance at the empty desk, and then Lemmy gave a quick shake of his head before replying. "Holb's got some regulars who he takes special care of. Guys who don't always have the money for a night's drinks. He extends a credit until they get paid again, and usually they make good. But - "

"But someone didn't," Raedrick finished for him.

Lemmy nodded.

"This has happened before?"

"Every now and then. Most times Holb gives 'em a reminder and it's all good. But once or twice we had to get the Dep - " He stopped and cleared his throat. "Your partner to make them live up to their word."

Raedrick felt his frown pulling at the scar on his chin. He wore a goatee now to conceal it, but he still felt it sometimes. Like now. "Who has reneged this time?"

"Stu Marly. He works the fishing boats. Payday was two days ago, and nothing. Holb sent me over to roust him this morning, and he slammed the door in my face."

"So now it's a matter for the law." Raedrick sighed and looked down at the parchment he had discarded. It was the report he was just finishing up for the Mayor, detailing his activities for the last month, and statistics on the various goings-on in town for the same period. It almost was more appealing than this squabble.

But, that was the job, most of the time. Petty disputes. It sure beat the alternative of fire and battle and things that threatened to bring Lydelton, and with it the entirety of Glimmer Vale, down to ruin. And there sure had been enough of those in the past year and a half.

He stood, the legs of his chair scraping across the polished planks of the Constabulary's floor. "I'll take care of it."

Lemmy bobbed his head. "Thanks, Constable."

Raedrick had dealt with Horace, the head of the Fishing Guild, a number of times over the course of his tenure as Constable. An older man, with a fully-grey head of hair and beard, who always wore a grey cloak and whose gruff demeanor only partially concealed a charitable heart, Horace had become quick friends with Julian when he and Raedrick first rode into town.

Raedrick's relationship with him had always only been professional. And he had found Horace to be a forthright and determined fellow. If sometimes headstrong.

"I've warned Stu about his drinking," Horace said as he clumped along Lydelton's main street beside Raedrick.

The Constable had sought Horace out first thing after leaving Lemmy. For one thing, he didn't know Stu at all, not even to look at him, let alone where he lived. For another thing, as a fishing man he looked up to Horace; they all did. He wasn't their boss, exactly. All the fishing men in Lydelton worked for the Covington brothers. But as head of the Guild Horace had pull with the brothers, and had negotiated a number of beneficial arrangements on behalf on the workers under his care. And he didn't hesitate to give them what for where the safety or health of his boys were concerned.

So there wasn't a fishing man in the town who wouldn't bend over backward for him.

In fact, several had done much more than that. When Raedrick and Julian first came to town and helped Lydelton repel a large group of brigands, at Horace's prompting a fair number of the fishing men had volunteered for martial training and then stood beside the two newcomers in battle against their town's foe.

It was always good to have Horace on your side, especially when dealing with the fishing men.

Raedrick looked at him sidelong as they followed the street northwest through town. "He hits it hard?"

Horace nodded. "Too hard, some days. Especially since Marta passed." He gestured to the right side of the intersection ahead, to the street that led to Bigsbe's Boarding House.

Turning in that direction, Raedrick as always felt the change beneath his feet, and fought back a minor bout of irritation.

Main Street was the only paved road in Lydelton; the others were packed earth that more often than not were muddy messes or worse, in the winter, treacherous ice sheets. He'd spoken with the Mayor about completing the project to pave the remaining streets in the town several times, and the answer was always the same: the reason Lydelton had stopped the project in the first place still held. Not enough money, and it required too much time away from the tasks that actually kept the town alive. Namely, fishing in Lake Glimmermere.

Which was understandable. But it still rankled, sometimes.

But that was neither here nor there right this moment. "Marta was his wife?"

Horace shook his head. "No, Sabine passed ten years ago. Marta was their daughter. Caught consumption the winter before you and Julian got to town."

Raedrick winced. He had always known that was a terrible blow to endure. But now, with his first child coming so soon… He couldn't imagine having to live through that.

"Poor guy."

Horace nodded. "One of the best men in the boats. But out of 'em…" He left off the rest of his sentence and shook his head again, this time in commiseration from the pitying expression on his face.

The two men walked in silence the rest of the two blocks until they reached Bigsbe's Boarding House.

It was a long, broad building, two stories tall with the sharply-angled tiled roofs that all of Lydelton had—the better to let snow fall off it during the winter. It took up most of block itself, and was well-kept.

Raedrick led the way through the front entrance and into the foyer, where Bigsbe's attendants held court behind a counter to the left of the front door.

The attendant today was Tami, a young girl just recently

reached maturity who still resided with her parents while she got herself onto her feet as an adult. She was almost pretty, and brown-haired with hazel eyes. But her smile made up for whatever deficiencies her bone structure had, turning her face into a pleasant ray of sunshine in the otherwise dimly-lit entryway.

She bobbed a curtsy when she saw Raedrick, the visible portion of her brown and white dress bunching slightly as she moved. "G'day Constable," she said. "How fairs Lani?"

Raedrick stopped, mention of his wife bringing a grin to his face. "Every day is a trial for her," he said. "And I thank the gods I don't have to endure it."

Tami giggled slightly, the same way all the young women did when Raedrick made that joke. It was only half a joke; he wasn't at all sure how he'd cope with the trials of pregnancy, let alone the pains of childbirth. But women were made for it, and knew in their bones how to cope. And they thought themselves superior to men because of it.

The fact that every woman batted their eyelashes when he made the statement proved it.

Oh well, whatever kept them happy.

"We're here to see Stu," Horace said, and Tami's smile faded. She glanced between the two of them and nodded, then gestured toward the rear of the foyer.

The room past the attendant's counter was split three ways: the stairs leading upward to the second floor and the two corridors leading left and right, providing access to the ground floor rooms.

Tami's fingers pointed to the right, and Horace nodded.

"Thanks," he said, but Raedrick was sure he didn't need the directions. There was no way Horace didn't know exactly where a member of his Guild lived.

They walked to the rear of the foyer and turned right. The corridor had matched pairs of doors every three paces all the way down to the end. Horace stopped at the third door on the left, and knocked.

No answer after a long several seconds.

Horace knocked again. Louder this time, with the heel of his fist.

Still nothing.

Horace turned to meet Raedrick's gaze, and his eyebrows rose slightly.

"He's not at work right?" Raedrick asked.

Horace shook his head. "He's got the evening shift. But he should be up by now."

"Try again."

More pounding, and still nothing.

Raedrick looked down the corridor, past the remaining three pairs of doors to where the corridor ended at the timber of the Boarding House's outer wall. "Wait here," he said, then he hurried back to the foyer, where Tami was doing sums behind her counter.

She jerked to attention when he stopped in front of her and rose to her full height. She was remarkably tall. Then she bobbed a curtsy yet again.

No time for this. Raedrick said, "Has Stu departed at all today?"

Tami slowed as she rose from her curtsy, her eyebrow rising. "I haven't seen him."

"When did you come on duty?"

She glanced toward the front door, and shrugged. "Six bells this morning."

Raedrick did some quick sums in his head. That was almost five hours ago. If Stu had been on the evening shift on the boats, he would have gotten off the boat in the dead of the night, since the fish only bit at sunset and sunrise. A few hours for a later dinner and some drinking….there was no way he wasn't still here if he had come home before Tami had come on duty. And if he hadn't come home since she had…

Well, there was no chance of that, unless he was face down in the gutter somewhere. But Raedrick would have heard of his being in that condition already. The largest use he and Julian put to the cell block was for local drunks who'd passed out some-where, so they could have a safe place to sleep it off.

Which meant Stu had to be in his room.

"Thank you Tami," Raedrick said. "Give Bigsbe my apologies."

He turned and hurried back to the corridor toward Stu's room, Tami's "What?" echoing behind him, unanswered.

Horace was still standing in front of the door, pacing impa-tiently. He looked up as Raedrick approached, eyes narrowed in concern.

"Break it down," Raedrick ordered.

Horace's eyes widened, then he turned and drove his heel against the door, at the level of its latch.

It sprang open inward, and the older man stumbled forward out of Raedrick's view.

He heard Horace curse softly, then cry out in shock. Then…

"Oh gods! Help, Raedrick!"

Raedrick sprinted the last few yards to the door and leapt inside.

The room was small, as he knew all the rooms at Bigsbe's to be. A bed just large enough for one on the right hand wall. A wash basin and chamber pot at its head. A small bureau on the other side of the room. A single window, with limp grey drapes that were drawn to blot out the view of the street beyond.

And in the middle, stood Horace. His arms were braced around the waist of a man Raedrick didn't recognize. But he wore the same grey cloak that Horace always did—the mark of a fishing man. Beneath the cloak, his shirt was yellow and his leggings green. He hung limply, his arms and legs dangling and his head lolling forward.

A rope was tied off around the rafter above his head, the other end looped around Stu's neck.

As Raedrick drew up, shocked, Stu's arms and legs spasmed weakly. Horace was pushing upward on his body, to try to relieve the pressure on his neck. But he was very nearly gone.

Raedrick sprang forward onto the bed and pulled his knife

from its sheath on his belt. He reached up and began sawing at the rope, desperate terror lending extra speed to his strokes.

Raedrick squared his shoulders and stepped into Holb's Tavern.

It wasn't really a building. Or, there was a building there. It stretched back from the street a ways until a twenty foot section of the red-painted building's wall had been cut away. In its place, Holb had installed a running countertop where he served drinks. He had erected a wooden awning above the bar that ran out a good thirty feet from the side of the building. Beneath that awning were a number of tables where Holb's customers could sit and drink. And eat, if they brought it with them. Holb did not serve food.

Raedrick had only come here a few times, and only then for business. His experience the first time he'd come through still weighed on him.

He hoped Holb's wife had gotten over the insult. But he hadn't even known it would *be* an insult...

Holb himself was a tall fellow with shoulders that put a giant to shame. He kept his head bald, whether because he preferred shaving it that way or because his hair had fled at his tempter Raedrick didn't know for sure. He had a scar that ran from his left eyebrow to his left ear, which had a little notch cut out of it, and he had dark brown eyes that shown with intelligence. And bad temper.

He held court behind the bar in his stained white apron, and cast a distrustful gaze upon Raedrick as he weaved his way through the tables. Even at this afternoon hour, Holb had plenty of customers.

"I found Stu," Raedrick said, without preamble, and Holb's eyebrow lifted, voicing a question without asking it.

"He tried to hang himself. He's over at the Healing Circle. Master Sebastini is tending to him."

Holb's jaw dropped open, shock followed by confusion followed by remorse crossing over his face in half a heartbeat before he got himself back under control.

"Ya get my money?" he said.

Raedrick scowled. "That's all you're worried about? His bar tab?"

Holb shrugged. "Rest of it's not my business."

Raedrick had to force himself to not clench his fists. "You know about his wife and daughter."

Holb nodded.

"Do you know what today is?"

Hold just looked at him with a blank expression.

Raedrick ground his teeth for a moment before continuing. "Today is his daughter's naming day. She would have reached her ascendancy this year."

Still nothing from the bartender.

"He's been coming here for years. You had to know."

"What's your point, Constable?" Hold said.

"How much did you let him drink last night?"

"His usual."

"And the night before that?"

"The same."

Raedrick felt that scar tugging at his chin again, and knew he was scowling too hard. But he didn't care. "I ought to arrest you for complicity in his death."

Holb snorted. "You already said he ain't dead. Don't play games with me Constable. We both know how that will turn out."

That took a bit of the wind from Raedrick's sails. Though it pained him to remember, Holb had an embarrassingly easy time throwing him out of the bar the first time. Raedrick had no desire to repeat that incident. And unless he was willing to draw steel, he suspected he would, if it came to blows.

And maybe even if he did draw steel.

"You knew he was having problems. And you let him drown himself in beer every chance he got. Even extended credit to him.

I know what he owed you. A fishing man couldn't pay that back in a year on his wages, not unless he went without food and shelter." Raedrick leaned forward. "What were you doing with him?"

Holb stopping moving. He just looked at Raedrick without words for a long moment. Then he shrugged.

Raedrick let out a disgusted snort. Fishing around inside his jacket, he pulled out a sack. It jingled as he held it up in front of the bar. And it ought to; he'd filled it with funds from the Constabulary's discretionary fund.

Raedrick tossed the pouch onto the bar, and it landed with a tinkling thunk. Holb's eyes twitched down toward it for the shortest of instants before returning back to Raedrick's. His left eyebrow moved upward slightly.

"That should even things up," Raedrick said. "But Stu never drinks here again."

Holb's right eyebrow rose to join the left.

"Master Sebastini thinks he will pull through, and he's putting Stu on a regime to purge him of his need for drink. But for that to work he has to abstain." He leaned toward Holb, locking stares with the big bartender. "I hear he's had even a single drink here, there will be problems."

Holb matched his gaze, and they stared into each other's eyes for what felt like a long time. Finally, after a small eternity, the bartender broke the connection, and reached down to pick up the pouch of coins. He tossed it in his hand, feeling the weight, then nodded. Though he was frowning slightly something about his carriage suggested satisfaction to Raedrick.

"However you want it, Constable," Holb said.

"Good."

With that, Raedrick turned and walked away from Holb's Tavern.

His report to the Mayor technically didn't have to include the information on the incident with Stu. It could go in the next month's report, and he wouldn't have to change a thing that he'd already written.

But Raedrick felt strongly that he needed to include it now. He might forget some detail, or forget the incident entirely. And that wouldn't be right. Not for Stu, not for his lost wife and daughter, not for Holb. And not for himself.

As Raedrick put pen to parchment on his desktop again, he reflected that he might have been too harsh with Holb. Yes, Holb knew what had happened with Stu's family. But that didn't mean his extending credit to the man was a malicious act. Maybe that was the only way he knew to help, or to at least show a bit of kindness to the man he'd known for years.

That was possible.

But it was certain that the outstanding debt had allowed Holb to gain some leverage over Stu. To do what, Raedrick had no idea.

Maybe nothing. Or maybe something. Something important.

Or not.

Raedrick shook his head at his flights of fancy, and wrote on, determined not to include those flights of fancy in his report. Just the facts, and only the facts. And the fact was that Stu was going to be fine. And now that he couldn't drink from Holb's tavern anymore, maybe he could become better than fine.

Maybe he'd get his life back together and going in a good path from now on.

Raedrick was beginning to smile a satisfied smile when it occurred to him that Holb's wasn't the only place in town Stu could get drink. He could just as easily go to -

The door latch lifted and the door to the outside swung inward. A figure stepped awkwardly in, and Raedrick saw long blond hair, well-formed breasts beneath a blue blouse and a white apron...

And a bulging belly, with baby about come any time now.

"Lani!" He bounded to his feet, coming around the desk before his wife could close the door behind herself. "Are you well?"

She gave him a level look. "Of course I'm well. Figured you'd be hungry; it's past dinner."

Lani extended her hands, and Raedrick blinked to realize he had completely missed the tray she was holding in her hands. He had focused in on her belly, and then up on her sweet face, so completely... But how could he have missed the scents rising from the plate atop the tray?

Fried fish, and broiled potatoes, and leeks, and...

His stomach growled, but Raedrick forced himself to dignity, accepting the tray quickly but steadily and turning to place it atop his desk. Then he paused to inhale the vapors rising from the meal.

"Your mother's outdone herself today," he said.

Lani snorted. "You say that every day."

He turned back to her and grinned. "It's true every day. Have you eaten?"

She nodded, but, rubbing her baby bump, she said, "But I may share of bit of yours if you don't mind."

He just grinned at her.

Along the wall adjacent to the front door were several chairs for guests, or witnesses. He moved one over in front of his desk and waited for her to sit down, then he took his own seat behind the desk.

They dug in.

After the initial couple minutes of biting and chewing, Lani said, "I heard about Stu."

Raedrick stopped in mid-chew, the nodded. Swallowing quickly, he said, "I was going to come talk to you and Molli about that. Ravi Sebastini is treating him, but once he's done he cannot have drink any more. Holb's already agreed not to let him have anything. You need to make sure he doesn't partake from The Carlock."

Lani nodded. "Mother and I already talked about it, soon as

we heard. He'll get no drink from us." She paused, then added. "Poor man."

Raedrick nodded, his eyes going downward again toward the bump in Lani's belly. "I can't imagine going through what he did."

She pressed her hand to her belly and nodded. "It's something we should have addressed a long time ago. But he seemed to take it all so well. And then..." She trailed off, and shook her head. "If there's one thing I love about this place, is that we all come together when its needed. We all help each other. Now that we really know, we'll make sure Stu gets back to healthy again."

Raedrick nodded. He had seen that instinct himself, back when he'd first visited Glimmer Vale as a child, and then again when he and Julian returned to find the town under siege by Isenholf's brigands. The sense of community, that they were all in it together, was striking. And he had seen it again several times since then.

So as he finished dinner with his wife, though he continued feeling pity for Stu, he didn't lack hope for the man. He would have a better future. They would all see to that.

And that would make a better future for them all.

MAILING LIST

If you enjoyed this book and would like word on new releases and special deals from Michael Kingswood, sign up for his newsletter on his website. Guaranteed to be spam-free, you can opt out at any time. And you can rest assured he will not share your information with anyone, for any reason.

https://michaelkingswood.com/newsletter-signup/

MEMBERSHIP

Michael would like to invite you to become a supporting member of his website. Similar in concept to Patreon, a few dollars a month will give you access to exclusive content, and help him to focus more of his time to writing fun and exciting stories for your enjoyment.

Sign up at his website:

https://www.michaelkingswood.com/membership/join/

ABOUT THE AUTHOR

Michael Kingswood is 20-year veteran of the US Navy submarine force and a lifelong fan of science fiction and fantasy literature. His work has appeared in numerous collections and anthologies, to include the Fiction River Anthology series from WMG publishing. He holds a bachelors degree in Mechanical Engineering as well as a Master of Engineering Management and a Master of Business Administration. He has four children and currently resides in San Diego.

Find Michael Kingswood online at:

www.michaelkingswood.com

gab.com/michaelkingswood

rumble.com/michaelkingswood

https://www.youtube.com/
channel/UCCpaDm2_p8HrVtLiejs98Gg

DAWN OF ENLIGHTENMENT

Masters Of The Sun

NOVELLAS

What Lurks Between

The Necromancer's Lair

The Champion

Veritas Morte

STORY COLLECTIONS

Tales Of Adventure #1

Tales Of Adventure #2

Short Story 10-Pack

A Jar Of Mixed Treats

Short Mystery 10-Pack

Stories From Glimmer Vale, Volume 1

SHORT FICTION

Michael has also published a number of shorter works, links to which can be found on his website.